F
JOH
JOHNSON, ANNABEL
 A golden touch

DATE DUE			
			ALESCO

4353

A GOLDEN TOUCH

A
GOLDEN
TOUCH

by Annabel & Edgar Johnson

Harper & Row, Publishers

New York and Evanston

For
Elizabeth and Abe James

Contents

PART I

DUST

One

The stagecoach bumped and lurched through the gathering dusk. On either side the craggy heights were being swallowed up by darkness, but Andy could still feel them there. The mountains were fiercer than he had ever imagined.

And he had done a good deal of imagining these past two weeks since it was settled that he would be sent here. Out on the flat prairies of Kansas, where he had lived all his life, he had heard the farmers talk about this steep, wild country. On rainy days, as they sat around the cracker-barrel in Grandpa's store, they had spilled yarns about the mine camps—the fights and friends and danger there. But mostly about gold.

Andy had been thinking of that. He knew what it looked like. He had seen the nuggets—the lustrous small lumps of pure precious metal. Most of the men who hung around Grandpa's store had done some panning at one time or another. They had told him how it was done: You scoop up a pan full of gravel, wash away the sand and pebbles, and the gold is left in the bottom. He thought he would just try that. Or dig a "glory hole." They had told him that men had got rich just by digging a hole in the ground. Keep on going down until you strike "color." If you're lucky. It made Andy's heart pump faster inside him, because he *thought* he felt lucky.

Squaring his shoulders and sitting up a little straighter, he glanced around at the other passengers—four men and a stout lady in a yellow shawl. She had got on at the last stop and had been eying Andy anxiously, the way women always do when they see a boy out on his own alone. He didn't want to encourage her. He wanted to talk to the men.

"How's it going around Black Hawk these days?" he asked offhand. "Pretty good pickin's?"

The fellows looked at each other soberly. One said, "Well, you might say 'tis. You swing a pick nine hours a day, draw your pay, and the Black Hawk gamblers pick it off of you."

Another cut in, "Main thing is, watch out they don't pick you up in an alley with a knife in your gizzard."

Andy had taken plenty of joshing around the store— he never let it bother him. But he had come to know that when men have to make their little jokes there is no point in talking sense to them. He was about to lapse into his private thoughts again when the lady burst out, as if a kettle had finally boiled over.

"Well, I think it's outrageous!" she said to everyone. "Letting a youngster go off to a place like Black Hawk all by himself!"

The men shuffled their feet uncomfortably as if she were scolding them. Andy felt called upon to pacify her.

"It's all right, ma'am. My father's expecting me." He said it with more confidence than he really felt. The fact was that he didn't know how he was going to recognize his father when he saw him. But he certainly wasn't going to tell her that.

"So young!" she fretted, plucking at the shawl. "What grade of school are you in, honey?"

"Eighth, ma'am." That was stretching a point, but it would have been the eighth next year. A twinge of homesickness came over Andy; his teacher had really been sorry to see him leave. Not that he was much good at arithmetic, but he had saved her canary's life. At least she thought so. She had almost cried when he told her he was going away for good. A nice woman—she never pestered him as the stout lady was doing right now.

"Have you had enough to eat? You don't look warm enough—it's dreadful cold for June. Did your mother make you wear your long underwear?"

It was such a personal sort of question, Andy floundered around and blurted out the truth before he could stop. "I haven't got a mother."

"Oh, you po-o-or boy!" She let out a groan and was probably going to ask more questions when one of the men passengers cleared his throat and began to talk briskly about the weather.

Andy was just as glad to be let out of the conversation. He didn't want to have to explain how his mother had died when he was born. It made him feel sorry inside, and somehow cheated, even though Grandma and Grandpa had been kind as could be all these years they had been raising him.

But he especially didn't want to have to explain about his father. Grandpa had made it sound reasonable—that a single man living in a tough gold camp couldn't take care of a little boy. Andy didn't blame his father at all —he really didn't. Never a Christmas had passed but that money came to pay for his keep. And a while back— when the calendar turned over a big page and it was 1900 instead of the old, familiar 18—something—his father had sent a brand new five-dollar gold piece wrapped in a scrap of paper on which he'd written, "For A." Andy had saved that.

For a long time, when he was younger, Andy had sort of expected him to come for a visit. Every time summer came around and other kids went fishing with their own fathers, he had gone off by himself and imagined how it would be—they would laugh a lot and like each other. Once he had even suggested to Grandpa that they might invite his father to come. But the old man had put down the notion.

"I don't know your pa well enough for that," he had

said vaguely. He never was one to care much for strangers.

So Andy had stopped wishing—he would have settled for a letter. Then when he got on in school he could see that it wasn't so easy to compose a piece of writing like a letter. Even Grandpa hardly ever did, except to order more stock for his store. And when, a month ago, he wrote the one to Andy's father, he had taken a long time over it, spelling the words carefully while Andy watched.

". . . I've been sick a long while. Got to sell the store and go into the Civil War Veterans' Home. Since Grandma passed on there's been no one to tend the house or cook. So I reckon you'll have to take Andy or he'll be sent to the orphanage. I'm sorry. . . ."

After that, Andy had tried to go about his chores without seeming to notice how the days dragged past. He wouldn't let himself think of all the awful things he had heard of orphanages. But secretly he was watching every stage for mail. When the answer came at last, it was just two lines of hard, black, square handwriting: "Send the boy along. I'll meet him at the stage station."

Not exactly a warm sort of note. And when Grandpa wrote back, giving the date of Andy's arrival, they had no further word. The old man had shaken his head once.

"Never could figure your pa out."

Andy wondered what his father did—whether he owned a gold mine maybe? Or was he a businessman, a storekeeper? A lawyer or something? Grandpa didn't seem to know either. Not that it mattered. All Andy

7

really wondered was whether now—now that he was practically grown, almost—wouldn't his father maybe be sort of glad to see him?

The stage had begun to bucket along faster. The passengers were stretching, starting to put on their overcoats. One of the men winked at Andy.

"This is it, sonny. Comin' into Black Hawk. Toughest gold camp west of Denver."

"In a pig's eye it is," another argued. "Cripple Creek is so much tougher it makes Black Hawk look like a tenderfoot town."

They jawed at each other good-naturedly, but Andy wasn't paying any attention. He had put on his farmer-style straw hat and the sheeplined coat and picked up his knapsack. He hadn't let the driver put that on top with the other folks' luggage, because it held everything in the world he owned—his extra clothing, his collection of arrowheads, and other personal possessions. And his money. Nine dollars and forty cents. It had taken quite awhile to save that, and now he had the gold piece and the other four dollars hidden between the inner lining and outer cover of the knapsack. The four dimes were in his bag of marbles. It wasn't much, but he hoped it would see him through any emergencies.

Such as might happen if his father couldn't—for some reason—meet him. After all, it was pretty late. He peered out the window into the darkness and saw lights ahead. More lights than any Kansas town would have shown at this hour.

As they passed the first buildings the driver began to

whoop and yell as if the fiends were on his tail, cracking the whip over the plunging horses. Down the narrow street they tore, past a row of swaybacked buildings that leaned against each other drunkenly. Bright paint, crude signs lit by gaslights—all flashed past in a blur of gaudy color. Snatches of laughter and brawling and dance-hall music mingled with the rattleclap of the stage as it jounced along. And then the driver hauled on the brake; they pulled up in a cloud of dust at the stage station.

Andy thought it was a dreadful commotion to make in the middle of the night. But as he climbed down out of the coach he saw that the board sidewalks were crowded with people. The town was as wide-awake as if it were noon. A number of men—tough, bearded miners—had moseyed over to watch the passengers get off. Greetings were being hollered back and forth.

As Andy looked around, hanging onto his knapsack hard, the stout lady climbed down and beckoned to the stationmaster. "This little lad is traveling alone," she said loudly. "Now you just take care of him until he's met."

Andy felt himself blush as the men all stared at him. The stationmaster came over.

"Somebody expecting you, young fellow?"

"Yes, sir. My father—William Brett."

A stillness came over the crowd. The stationmaster looked troubled. "Well now," he muttered. "Will-yum Brett . . ."

A whisper rustled through the onlookers. "He says he's Billy Brett's kid!"

Suddenly a grizzled miner let out a short, angry laugh.

"Ain't that a shame! Who'd have thought Brett would have a young'un?"

The stationmaster turned to try to hush him up, but the big fellow shoved on past, striding over to look down at Andy, not unkindly, but grim.

"Boy's bound to find out sooner or later. Sonny, you're lookin' for your papa in the wrong place. He don't live here no more."

"He said he'd meet me," Andy insisted as firmly as he could, with his stomach beginning to turn over inside him.

"Likely he meant to, but I reckon his plans got changed sort of sudden. Tell the truth, we had to—so to speak—ask him to de-part from this-here town a few days ago."

A rough voice from the crowd called out, "And I say let's send the brat packin', too, if he's kin to Billy Brett. I got skinned out of a month's pay by that double-dealin' card shark."

The miner swung around, glaring at them all. "And I say leave the kid alone. It ain't his fault his papa's a crook."

Two

Andy felt numb. It all seemed unreal—these strange people and what they were saying. He heard it, but it didn't quite get through to where he could feel it yet.

The stout lady was insisting, "I'll take the poor child home with me!"

The stationmaster shook his head, irritated. "No need, ma'am. I reckon we can take care of him, seein' it was us ran his pa out of town."

Meanwhile the burly miner had taken off the hard helmet he wore—a curious dome-shaped hat with a number of nicks in it. Turning it upside down, he dropped some coins into it and passed it to the crowd. It took Andy a minute to realize they were taking up a collection for him. He began to stammer a protest, but now their attention was diverted by a new ruckus just down the street.

Another group of men was marching toward the station—an angry-looking bunch led by a big, handsome fellow in a white Stetson. He wore a sheriff's star and was holding a shotgun pointed at another man, herding him along like a prisoner. This one was slender and dark, his face shadowed by a flat-crowned black hat. He walked warily, his hands hanging loose as if ready to fight, though he wore no weapons. Straight on up to the stage station they came, while a hush fell over the crowd. They could even hear what the sheriff was saying as they came up.

"This cock-eyed story of yours had better be true, Brett!"

Someone in the sheriff's posse bellowed, "Let's string him up—we told him we would if he came back."

As the group stopped before the stationmaster, the sheriff didn't notice Andy. Fingering the shotgun, he spoke angrily.

"We just picked this bird up sneaking along a side street. He's got some unlikely story that he's come here to meet his son."

But Andy was looking at the prisoner, who had seen him at once. Silently they stared at each other, and a qualm of recognition came over the boy. Those lean features and dark brows were almost like the ones he saw in his own mirror every morning. But hard—jaw as hard as a flint arrowhead. And the eyes he couldn't read.

The stationmaster was saying softly, "Why don't you carry that scattergun a little easier, Duke? It's no story—the boy is here."

Brett walked away from them now to come over to Andy. "Where's your baggage?" he asked quietly, his lips hardly moving.

"This is all I've got." Andy showed him the knapsack.

"Then come on. We're not welcome here." As he turned away he looked once at the sheriff. Andy saw fury and bitterness and contempt in that glance. Then the crowd drew back silently to let them pass.

The sheriff seemed dissatisfied, but made no move to stop them. "You've run your luck to the end of the string, Billy," he called as they walked away. "No excuses next time. Git and stay got."

The plump lady was moaning. "It's a crime, that's what it is, to let an innocent child go off with a man like that!"

Will Brett's somber eyes were fixed dead ahead and his expression was blank. Andy tried to cover up his own nervousness with a rigid face but couldn't help wondering if that shotgun was pointed again at their backs. He was glad when they passed the last lighted buildings and were alone, walking through the night.

A half-dozen times he started to speak. He thought he should thank his father for coming. He wanted to say something confident, but couldn't think of anything that would sound true. He wondered where they were going, but decided not to ask. From pure uneasiness he began to whistle.

Out of the darkness William Brett spoke softly. "You happy about something?"

"N-no. I mean—yes, sir. I'm glad I'm here." It sounded pretty lame, even to Andy.

"May be the sorriest day of your life. I'm afraid you'll wish you were in that orphanage yet."

Silence settled in again. Andy was careful not to whistle. He really had no gumption to, anyhow. He felt tired—too tired to figure it all out. It was so different from the way he had pictured it.

"What did they tell you?" his father asked at last. "How much did they say?"

"I don't know—something about cards. I didn't understand it."

"You'd be no son of mine if you were slow to grasp a thing."

And it came home to Andy all at once that this really was his own father. Almost dazed, he repeated the thought aloud. "Yes, sir, I'm your son." And then realizing that he sounded a little dismayed, he hurried on to add, "I'm glad to meet you, sir."

It only seemed to make his father more bitter. With remote mockery he said, "What kind of raising did your grandfather give you—to be pleased to meet a gambler who's been caught dealing off a stacked deck?"

"He raised me not to believe everything I hear." Andy held his breath, hoping that the man beside him would take this moment to say it was all some mistake—that he had been wronged and was really innocent. But no word came from the shadowy figure at his elbow. At last, almost desperately, Andy burst out, "Anyhow, they say Black Hawk is a bad town. I reckon there'll be some better place to live."

"Could be worse, too," his father said, with that grim humor. "We'll see if you've still got all that stiff upper lip a few days from now. You may as well know—I'm broke. When they run a man out of town they seldom allow him time to settle his affairs. There's not so much as a can of beans to eat tomorrow, and we've got not even a tent to put over our heads tonight. You may find it slightly uncomfortable, sleeping on a gravel bed. As for where we're going only the Lord knows, but wherever it may be we'll go afoot. I just hope you like to walk, boy."

Three

Andy was dreaming—not sleep-dreaming, but drifting in a wakeful sort of doze behind tight-shut eyes. During these past long hours of the night he had considered everything he knew in the world and gone back over it twice. His father had been right about one thing: gravel makes a mean bed.

It sounded like morning now—birds were beginning to chatter. But Andy was too stiff and cold to open his eyes. Lying with his knees drawn up under his coat, the collar turned up as far as it would go around his ears, and his head pillowed on his knapsack, he dreamed of the loft above the store. The odor of food coming up from below, the sweet clean straw that made his mattress and the warmth of the animals that always shared his blankets.

There were always quite a few little creatures around

the loft. The raccoon that he had found with its leg broken in that trap; and the little chewed-up cat that the coyotes had chased up a tree—he always seemed to happen along just when something needed help. Grandpa never minded if he brought them home and mended them up—not even the little garter snake or the turtle with the cracked shell. Not that he had let *them* in bed with him, but the furry things usually found their way under the covers on a cold morning. He lay still, missing them all fiercely, wondering where they were now. Of course, they could take care of themselves by the time he had turned them loose. He just hoped he could manage as well himself.

When he heard someone come over to his side, he didn't move until a cheerful voice said, "Maybe the lad's froze." A hand touched his shoulder and Andy opened his eyes groggily. It gave him quite a shock. For a minute he got mixed up between dream and reality, and thought he was looking up at the raccoon—dark-rimmed eyes, long beautiful fur, and the sniffy little nose. Then his head cleared and he realized it was a man. Wearing horn-rimmed glasses and a cap of brown fur, with a curling mustache on his upper lip, he had a comic face almost as bright and curious as an animal's.

"Up and at 'em, nephew! Sun's rising—it'll get the chunks of ice out of your blood."

Stiffly Andy sat up. It was broad daylight and he could see better where he was, though it hardly cheered him. The land was harsh and rocky, a big gravelly valley between steep hillsides that were dotted with huge boulders. Nearby, a stream churned between its banks, high with spring runoff. When Andy went over to splash some water on his face, he found it to be ice-cold. Shivering, he went back to the fire where his father was seated on a rock. The man with the glasses was heating something in a tin can—it smelled a little like coffee— and talking along in that brisk tone.

"It was the best I could do. The hotel uses an abominable brand of Java and these grounds were not at their freshest when I acquired them from the pot last night. Well, nephew, here you are! Just in time for breakfast."

Andy's father seemed plunged in thought too deep to notice him, but the other man was holding out the can of steaming brew. Andy drank a little; it was mighty thin, but the warmth helped drive off the chill. He was acutely hungry, though.

Diffidently he suggested, "I've got a sandwich in my knapsack. I didn't want it for lunch yesterday. Maybe we should eat it now."

"Fortuitous!" exclaimed this man who, apparently, was his uncle. "You hear that, Billy? The lad has come to us bearing edibles."

"Be still, Hep," Brett said moodily. "I'm trying to think what to do."

Andy went to get the sandwich; it was made of good, thick slabs of ham and cheese. When he had brought it to the fire, his uncle sliced it judiciously three ways.

"Here, Billy, you'll think better on a full stomach."

Teasingly he thrust the bit of food into Brett's hand. "Eat hearty and cheer up. I gathered some useful equipment last evening while you were engaged with our friend, the sheriff."

Andy's father began to eat slowly. "I wondered where you were."

"Oh, I wasn't far off. But I thought since they had caught one of us, the other should stay conveniently at large, pending nasty developments. When I saw that I wasn't going to have to rescue you, I lingered on in town a bit. Several old friends owed me favors—I thought I'd just collect from them."

"The same way you 'collected' the coffee grounds?" Brett asked distantly.

Hep looked injured. "I'd not have supposed you would be critical of my little efforts to help our sorry situation, Billy. It wasn't me that got us into this, y'know. I'm the victim of cold misfortune, for no other reason than that I'm kin to you, so it hardly behooves you to find fault."

"I just don't want Duke coming after us—not right now." Brett shot a glance at Andy.

"Nor I! Nor I!" Hep was unwrapping a big odd-shaped package. "That's why I thought a few tools might hasten us on our way to new parts. Can't pan gold with your bare hands. So—" he set forth two large shallow metal dishes the size and shape of a frying pan without a handle.

Brett looked skeptical. "This stream's long since been

worked out. There's nothing in there bigger than dust."

"That's why I acquired this"—Hep took a vial of some liquid from his pocket—"and this." From another pocket he drew a large potato. "We're in business, brother."

Andy expected his father to make some new discouraging remark but he only shrugged and got to his feet. "In that case, let's get at it. No, you stay here and tend the fire, boy."

Hep caught Andy's crestfallen look and seemed to sympathize. "That is to say, unless you want to learn the fine art of panning for gold?"

"Yes, sir!" he nodded quickly. "I'd like to."

"In that case, much as it grieves me, I'll lend you my equipment." His uncle winked, and Andy grinned back. He was beginning to feel better by the minute.

As they went down to the stream, Brett was silent and disapproving, but made no further objection. Hep put the big pan in Andy's hands and showed him how to scoop up the gravelly stream bed—rock, water, sand, and all—in a muddy mess.

"Roil it good first, twist the pan back and forth so the water swirls around; shuck the whole works up and down so that the rocks keep turning over. That's it, keep 'em moving. Remember, nephew, gold is heavy, it'll settle to the bottom if you give it the chance. Now, as the stones turn over, begin to flick 'em out of the pan with your thumbs. So—"

With Hep coaching, Andy began to get the hang of

it, sloshing the water back and forth, skimming the loose gravel over the edge of the pan little by little.

"Excellent, my boy. Keep it up till there's only black sand left in the bottom, then put the sand in this." Hep gave him a tin can. "When you get that full, bring it to me. I'll be up by the fire."

Left alone, with good work to occupy his hands, Andy tried to think more clearly about all this. Secretly he watched his father, who was hunkered down by the stream just below. He handled his pan skillfully, yet it seemed hardly the right work for him. His hands were so well groomed, his clothes so fine, in spite of their wrinkles. They must be gamblers' clothes, Andy thought —a black broadcloth suit with a yellow vest over a white shirt, and a small narrow black tie. The flat-crowned black hat was shoved back on Brett's head; the lanky dark hair fell forward in his eyes exactly like Andy's own cowlick. It disturbed him a little—to see someone look so much like him, someone so strange.

He felt much more at home with this new-found uncle. He seemed friendly enough, letting Andy use his gold pan, teaching him this valuable knack, giving him the first chance to test whether he really had a "golden touch."

Not that Andy was going to tell anybody about it, but his teacher had said he must have been born with one. Of course, she was talking about something else— how he had saved her canary and so forth. But when she had explained the term and told him the story of the old Greek king, it was evident to Andy that a golden touch was no joke. What the king had touched turned to gold—real gold. And as soon as Andy had learned he was coming to these mountains he had begun to wonder if maybe he really might have been born with some special kind of luck.

With red, numb fingers he tipped the last of the water out of the pan. He almost expected to see a nugget there, even though this was only his first try. Shifting the pan back and forth, he surveyed the thin layer of black sand with disappointment. A few tiny bright specks, but nothing you could even try to pick up in your fingers. He couldn't see much point in keeping it, but did as Uncle Hep had told him and emptied the sand into the tin can. At this rate it was going to take quite a while to fill it. Hastily he dug down into the cold stream again, scooping another heavy panful of muddy gravel and water.

After the first hour of panning Andy began to feel hollow inside. And not so much as a flake of gold to show for it. By the end of the second hour he was nearly caved in. Something about the swollen coldness of his hands was drawing all the heart out of him. And his knees felt as if they were full of needles. When he saw his father coming up the bank toward him, he wasn't sure he could get uncrouched.

Brett looked down at him out of that expressionless face. The deep-set eyes were probing, and far back in their depths Andy glimpsed emotions that frightened him a little. "Had your bellyful yet? Maybe next time you'll be readier to do as I say, stay by the fire and keep warm."

Andy scrambled up hastily, embarrassed to think that he had ignored his father's orders the very first time. "I'm sorry, sir. I just thought this would be a good thing to learn."

"So you flounder around while your uncle takes his ease. Did it occur to you that he might do it faster and better? The point is for us to get on our feet as quickly as we can."

It was true. Andy felt a panicky sense of failure in all directions. He had disobeyed and had no results either. He tried to stammer some sort of excuse. "I thought— I mean I hoped I'd find some gold but—" Then, on a sudden inspiration, he burst out. "But I can help! I've got some money—it's in my knapsack." He broke off before the fierceness of his father's look.

"That'll be a fine day, when I ask a kid to stake me!" For a minute he stared at Andy with taut violence, as if he might even strike him. Finally, stiff as a strange dog circling a pup, he went over and picked up Andy's tin can which was still only half full of sand, filling it from his own. When he spoke, the cold mockery was back in his voice.

"Take this up to the fire. Listen and learn some more. If it's gold you came here after, there's not a man in the West who knows more about it than your Uncle Hep."

Four

Andy walked up the slope of the riverbank, still absorb-
ing the hurt of that word "kid." His father had seemed
angry because he was doing Uncle Hep's share of the
work—which he was. Andy knew it and had known it
all along. He supposed that made him look pretty foolish, but was it enough to warrant such a scolding?

Of course, the shame of being driven from a town in
disgrace was enough to turn a man bitter. But if Andy
had been given the least chance, he would have been
quick to say, "I know you didn't cheat anybody!
They're a bunch of liars!" And yet his father wouldn't
give him that chance, not the slightest opening.

It was hard to think through it, what with the rumbling of his stomach. The crisp, sunny morning, the
work and fresh air had given him a thriving appetite.
He was glad that Hep had managed to "collect" a po-

tato from somewhere. Oh, he understood that much of the talk this morning—Uncle Hep's "collecting" was very much like swiping things. But who would miss old coffee grounds, or one lone spud? Andy was just glad it was a big one. Maybe it was baking in the coals right now, though boiling would make it stretch farther.

Hep waved as Andy came up. "How's prospecting?"

"If black sand was worth money I'd be rich," Andy said ruefully.

"Well, we'll see—maybe you are, anyhow." Hep chuckled. Getting to his feet, he took the tin can, poured the sand into the gold pan, and put it over the fire. "Helps if she's dry."

Andy held his chilled hands toward the blaze. He hated to mention that potato, but—

"Now, then, where did I put my magnet?" Hep began to hunt through his pockets; brought forth a small horseshoe-shaped piece of iron with which he began to skim the surface of the sand. "Hope you keep plenty of odds and ends in your pockets, nephew. Life's full of emergencies."

"Yes, sir." Andy could certainly agree with that statement.

"See how it picks up the black iron?" Hep held out the magnet which was covered with clinging grains of sand. Cleaning it off, he began to rake the pan again. "Iron loves a magnet. Gold won't touch it—she's too choosy. Sit down, nephew, this'll take a while."

"Would you like me to peel the potato?"

"No, that won't be necessary." As they sat across the fire from each other Hep eyed him judiciously. "You're a good lad. Eager to help—an excellent trait."

"I wish my father"—Andy fumbled—"he doesn't seem to like me much."

Hep wiped the magnet again carefully before he spoke. "Billy's under a strain just now, my boy. Don't judge too quick. If he seems scornful, that's his natural way. Doesn't mean he dislikes you. Mercy, he acts the same to me, and I'm his best friend. Only one he's got just now."

"Well, I'd be his—I mean—I'd like to—"

Hep looked up from his work curiously.

In a rush Andy blurted out the question that had been gnawing him. "He didn't *really* cheat anybody at cards, did he?"

"Why—no—of course not." Setting down the pan, Hep took off his glasses and began to polish them busily. "I'm sure Billy wouldn't do a thing like that. You shouldn't even harbor such a doubt, my boy. Your father is one of the best poker dealers in this territory—he knows every trick there is, but I can tell you he'd never use 'em. I never saw an honester man, no-sir-ree!"

The more he kept talking, the more uneasy Andy felt. Because Uncle Hep sounded as though he wasn't entirely convinced himself. "Then why did the people in Black Hawk run him out?"

"That's a tough one, nephew. I'm bound to say they ran him out because he was dealing with a stacked deck of cards. That means they were arranged to fall in his favor. But—I say *but*—who stacked 'em? That's what I want to know."

Andy didn't get the drift of the question.

"Tell you what I think," Hep went on with a knowing wink. "I think Duke Dade—the sheriff, you saw him last night—I think Duke's behind this. He's had hard feelings against your pa for quite a while. There was a little matter up in Central City—no need to go into that. But the fact is, Duke's been spoiling to catch Billy doing something wrong. And if you ask me, it was an odd coincidence that Duke just happened to be in the Poker Palace the other night when all the—unpleasantness occurred. He was almighty quick to escort your pa out of town. He's a mean jasper, Duke is. I wouldn't put it past him to have planned the whole thing."

"How?" It sounded farfetched to Andy.

"Well, suppose he hired some sharper to throw the game in your pa's favor? Make it look as if Billy was doing a fast shuffle? It could happen. Here now, let's see—I'd say we've got most of the iron out of this batch."

Andy was glad to hear it. He hoped the next matter of business would be lunch. But Hep was taking the vial of liquid from his pocket. When he poured it into the pan with the handful of sand that was left, Andy saw it was mercury—the same stuff he had once rolled around in his palm when Grandpa's thermometer got broken. It stood out in beads in the sand, then raced around and around as Hep tilted the pan back and forth.

"Gold's the lady who loves fast company," he was going on cheerfully. "She's got an affinity for this slippery fellow—quicksilver. That means he can gather her to his bosom any time they're thrown together. Let's see what he's picked up." He made a pocket in the sand, and the mercury ran into it in one big quivering globule, which Hep collected deftly in the vial again.

Andy tried to seem interested, but the truth was that he was getting so hungry he could hardly sit still. He was relieved when his uncle took the potato out of his pocket.

"Contrary to current opinion, I was busy this morning." Hep picked up a round piece of cast iron—a stove lid—and set it on the fire. "Found that in an old deserted cabin up the river. I doubt the owner will ever need it again."

It seemed to Andy an unattractive thing to cook on, but at this point he wasn't about to be fussy. His mouth was already watering as Hep sliced the potato in half; then turned puzzled when his uncle went on to scoop a hole in the center of the cut side. Wasting some of it? Andy was beginning to squirm, when, to his consternation, Hep opened the vial and poured the mercury into the hole. Andy knew the stuff was supposed to be poison!

"Never try this in a closed room, my boy—" Using the tail of his coat to protect his hand, Hep picked up the hot stove lid, laid it flat atop the potato with its cup of mercury, then swiftly reversed the whole business so that the potato lay face down on the iron. Andy looked for the mercury to run out, but it didn't. Instead, there was a whiff of fumes, and when Hep lifted the potato away, the quicksilver was gone. Left in its place was a small mound of fine dust. In the sunlight it glinted with a dull lustre.

"And there," said Hep, "is your first gold. Congratulations, nephew."

To use Uncle Hep's word, it was a coincidence. Too much of one. Andy sat and fed sticks into the fire that afternoon, trying to ignore the aching, shriveled-up, empty feeling in his middle, and thinking gloomily of this inescapable coincidence. How could his teacher have come *that* near the truth with her story of the old Greek king?

Like all tales that you're told in school, the "golden touch" story had a grown-up type of moral tacked on it. The king found out you could get too much gold. When he had tried to eat a baked potato for supper, it had turned to gold in his mouth and he couldn't swallow it. Later on, he kissed his little daughter and *she* turned to gold—Andy never took this sort of thing seriously. But the potato part certainly bore an odd resemblance to what had happened this afternoon. They had some gold —Uncle Hep said they could sell it for $20.00 an ounce at the nearest Wells-Fargo office. But right now Andy was empty as a turned-up bucket and the potato was sure enough ruined.

Uncle Hep had got the mercury back out of it, all right. In fact it was amazing how, when the stove lid had cooled a little to just the right heat, the quicksilver came running back out and stood shimmying on the surface, so they could use it over again on the next batch of sand. His father and Uncle Hep were down at the stream right now, going at the panning as hard as they could. When they came back up they were going to use the other half of the potato to "retort" some more. He glanced toward the river and saw them coming. They seemed to be discussing something.

Hep's voice was high and excited—the words carried clearly to the fire. "Cripple Creek! That's the best idea yet! In just one month they took over two hundred thousand dollars' worth of gold from a single mine over there. They say the town is anybody's fair game!"

Andy saw his father shake his head. "We're not going there to play games."

Hep laughed out loud. "We'll see! We'll see! You've never backed down from one yet, Billy!"

Brett turned on him. "You fool! You brass-plated idiot—do you think it will ever be like that again? Haven't you got it through your head yet—?" The low words came, almost strangled with desperation—"I've got a *kid* now!"

Five

It was just as well, Andy thought, that they hadn't tried to hike to Cripple Creek. He didn't mind walking, but climbing up into these high mountains was something else. Besides, he had always dreamed of some day riding a train.

The caboose was a snug place—bunks one above the other on either side, a pot-bellied stove at the front end. The men were seated around it now; the early dawn air was cold. Will Brett seemed a world apart from the others—slumped in his chair, taciturn and brooding, while Uncle Hep and the trainman gabbed along. Although their talk was of gold, Andy had torn himself away to concentrate on the train ride.

He had found a perch halfway up the ladder at the far end of the caboose, watching out the window of the lookout box. It was just a small raised place in the top of the car, but it put him head and shoulders above the rest of the world.

The train looked a mile long as it snaked through the woodlands ahead. Over a hundred cars. Andy tried to picture how much gold ore it would take to fill them all. And the trainman said they took up that many empties every night, to be loaded at the mighty mines of Cripple Creek. Even the names he spoke had the ring of bigness —*The Independence, The Vindicator, The Portland, The Golden Cycle.* Andy could just hear what was being said if he listened; he could hear their voices quicken as they spoke of rich ore. High-grade, they called it.

Uncle Hep was saying, "That's for me! I read where one of those veins was six feet wide—pure gold. Fellow tossed his hat in the air and dug where she fell. Hit the vein smack in the middle."

"Sure, sure, it happened that way two or three times," the trainman said, "back in the old days ten years ago. Just don't swing your pick too quick, fellows. Every inch of Cripple Creek District is already staked. Why, there's so many mines, you can walk their tunnels clear from Cripple Creek town to Victor and never come aboveground."

Andy leaned down from the lookout box. "You mean we can't dig a hole of our own *anywhere?*" he asked anxiously.

"Oh, it can be arranged," the trainman called back over his shoulder. "Like I was saying, a handful of the big boys own it all, but they'll lease some of it to you. You have to sign papers saying you'll give 'em a percentage if you strike pay-rock."

"We're not going to Cripple Creek to prospect," Brett said quietly. "We're looking for jobs. I've heard there's work to be had."

"That's right. If you're a hard-rock man you can pick your shift. Seems like they can't get enough men to dig all this ore. Especially fellows who can work at high altitude. You boys ever bust rock at eleven thousand feet before? Makes you a mite woozy at first."

Eleven thousand feet was higher than Andy could imagine. But all night, as the train inched along up the long grade, he had lain in his bunk wakeful, feeling the tilt of the steep pull. Right behind the caboose a big brute of an engine snorted and roared, pushing the train from behind while four other engines struggled up ahead. Now as they lengthened out along a straight stretch of track, Andy could see them all. Black smoke poured from the stacks, and the huge wheels—the drivers—flashed in the first rays of morning sunlight.

The land was leveling off now; the train had picked up speed. At one little crossroads they passed, children were hanging on a fence to watch and count the cars. Andy waved at them—it was a lofty feeling. But when he saw a farm boy, bareback on a horse, herding some cattle out to pasture, a wave of homesickness came over him. His pleasure faded and he almost shuddered. For all its grandeur, the train was a fierce, thundering thing, taking him on and on at a steady rackety-click, away from the past and into a strange new world.

As they raced through a long cut, he saw up ahead a towering black structure like a giant scaffold, wide at the bottom and narrow at the top, where there was a big wheel hung with cables. Around the foot of the rickety-looking thing were grouped some dilapidated buildings of corrugated iron that had long since rusted, and to one side was a mound of worthless-looking green-ish rock. It all looked too junky to be anything important, but the tracks of the siding were polished bright with use. As they passed Andy could see back into the yard where switch engines were at work, moving cars full of more rock. Then when he glanced again at the scaffold, the big wheel began to spin—faster, faster, reeling up cable from the hole below it. From under-ground a huge bucket burst into sight and flipped over on its side to send rock crashing down a long chute. Quicker than the blink of an eye, it righted itself again and went plunging back into the hole. The train was past before Andy could realize that he'd just seen a gold mine at work.

As the trees gave way and the land opened out into a broad, rolling countryside, other scaffolds could be seen rearing their tall, harsh lines on the crests of the hills; mountains of dump rock reaching down toward the val-leys. Along the skirts of the dumps were tarpaper shacks of every description—Andy supposed people must live in them. He saw washing hung out to dry and dirty kids

34

playing amid the scatter of old broken machinery and torn sheet metal.

The train was winding right through the thick of it, past huge tin buildings aflame with rust, switchyards where locomotives chuffed back and forth, pouring their dirty smoke into the air. Some of the train tracks led right into the dark interiors of the big structures that looked like giant hay barns. On the side of one was painted in letters as tall as a man—EAGLE SAMPLER.

"Nope, sonny, they don't test bird feathers." The trainman had come up behind him on the ladder. "That shebang samples the ore from every trainload that goes out, to see how rich she's running. Now, if you don't mind giving me my job back, we're coming into Victor."

After the ramshackle world they had just come through, the town of Victor was something else again. A prosperous-looking place with respectable brick buildings and broad streets, there was the smell of gold about it, but a different flavor. Assay offices, banks, hotels, windows bearing the names of mine companies were on every side. Even the pawnbrokers' shops had a handsome appearance, displaying fine pocket watches and rings. Of course, it wasn't all so refined. There were enough saloons and dance halls to shock the whole state of Kansas.

As Andy and the two men passed a cardhouse the click of silver and murmur of laughter inside could be heard, though it wasn't yet eight o'clock in the morning.

35

Hep's head jerked around as he heard the sounds, but Brett just shoved his hands in his pockets and walked on a little faster. At the next corner he stopped. They were nearly to the edge of town.

"I'd say we've seen it," he said, "except for the back alleys, and they're all alike anywhere."

"A handsome little city," Hep observed happily. "I'd say we will do well here. Unless you want to take a look at Cripple Creek first?"

This was still a stumper to Andy. They were in Cripple Creek right this minute—the whole district was called that—but the town itself, for which all this was named, was seven miles away.

"I've heard it's a rich man's place. The bankers live there," Brett said.

"All the better!"

"All the worse. Prices will be high. Victor is a workingman's town and it's here we'll stay, if we can find some kind of rooms. The trainman said they're hard to come by and cost dear. After paying our way here we've not got enough cash to rent a piano box."

"I have," Andy reminded him. "Why couldn't we use some of mine, Father?" He faltered at the strange glance Brett cast at him.

"You'll need all yours to lease some land and start that gold mine," his father said mockingly. "Now listen to me, boy. Your uncle and I must go separate ways to search for work. You'll have to take care of yourself until tonight. Keep out of the alleys and don't talk to strangers. We'll meet back here on this corner at sundown."

Andy nodded, but Hep looked troubled. "If we're going to split up, Billy, how about divvying the cash? Seems like a long time since we ate those scrambled eggs on the train. And you're holding what's left of the money."

"I'm going to keep on holding it, too. If we don't eat lunch we can eat supper." Brett gave them a flip of his hand and walked off toward the long hill beyond town. Up there, a half-dozen mines sat amid their dumps.

Hep looked at Andy helplessly. "Nephew, I confess I don't always understand your father. He's a strange one—here he trusts you to keep these funds of yours that you say you have. But mine—ours—the return from that dust we all worked so hard to get—he takes it all, without a flicker of remorse. Hardly seems fair."

He looked so dismayed Andy felt a quirk of sympathy.

"Much as I hate to ask a new acquaintance such a favor," Hep was going on ruefully, "I was wondering if you might float a small loan for me. I promise you interest on your money—and by nightfall, too. It wouldn't take much—just enough for a small stake. There are days when you feel lucky."

The word touched deep into Andy's own private hopes. It was like sharing some secret with his uncle—it made him feel warmer, somehow more part of the family. In a burst of fellowship he grinned.

37

"Sure, I'll lend you some, sir." Unbuckling the knapsack, he felt down inside, between the inner and outer walls. Must have chosen the wrong side. Turning it around, he looked harder. But it was no use—the lining was empty. His money was gone.

Six

Blindly Andy walked along the streets of Victor, not watching—or caring much—which way he went. All around him were hustle and color. He felt buffeted by the noise—the crash of rock down the big chutes, the blast of train whistles, other whistles shrieking jets of steam from the tops of the mine buildings.

Men were streaming in and out of the gates as the shift changed. Hurrying, going somewhere, carrying their lunch buckets under their arms, hard helmets tipped back on their heads, and clothes all over rock dust, they crowded past. Andy walked against the tide, searching their faces.

All his life he had taken people for granted. The farmers out in Kansas were pretty much alike—sensible, quiet men. Oh, one might have more humor and another might be smarter than the rest. But it had never occurred to Andy to wonder much about what they were really like underneath. Now as he looked at the blur of faces in the throng he saw harsh lines and soft—weak mouths and strong ones. Eyes that slid away from you, others fixed straight ahead. Lean, mean faces and wary ones and stupid ones. Some were closed, like his father's.

He had begun to understand a few things about that. His father kept that mask on to hide behind. He used it to cover his impatience at having a boy to feed and look out for. Andy knew he must naturally resent having to change from one sort of life to another. But was it, too, to keep people from seeing a guilty conscience? Up to now Andy had doggedly refused to let any such doubt bother him. It was unthinkable—other people's fathers commit crimes, but not your own. He went over it all once more.

There must have been times when he had left the knapsack unwatched, but he couldn't remember any. Other people must have had the chance to steal from him, but he couldn't imagine who. What he did know was that only one person in the world knew the money was there. He tried to tell himself that somebody else could have guessed. Uncle Hep, maybe. But then why would he try to borrow the very money that was missing? Besides, he had looked as disappointed as Andy was. For a long minute he had stood there, sober. Then he smiled gloomily.

"Never mind, nephew. These things happen. It's a shifty world. Don't worry, we'll all be rich someday."

But ever since he had gone off and left Andy to his own dismayed thoughts, it kept boiling down to just one terrible suspicion. Even though maybe a man might be embarrassed to ask a kid to stake him, he might just feel that his son's money was as good as his, and not see anything wrong with taking it. Every time he faced the thought he screwed up with misery. All these years he had built a picture of his father—brave, knowing, and strong.

Sweating under his clothes, Andy sat down weakly on a hitch rail, shoved back his straw hat, and swiped at the moisture on his forehead. He felt a little sick and wondered if it could be this altitude the trainman had mentioned. He was aware that there was someone else sitting on the rail nearby, but didn't look around until a gravelly old voice roused him.

"What's the matter, skipper? You got a touch of catarrh? Have a pill." A scarred old hand, leathery with calluses, was thrust under his nose. It cradled a bright pink tablet.

Andy shook his head. "Thank you, no, sir."

The old man sniffed and shrugged and took the pill himself. "Good for catarrh," he mumbled, his lower lip sticking out as if he were hurt that Andy had turned him down. Something about him—the red-rimmed old brown eyes or the long yellow-white hair that grew down over his ears and neck, or the moistness of his nose—all at once it reminded Andy of Grandpa's ancient hound.

That dog was always ailing. Never was such a one for hurt feelings either. If anyone treated him like a dog he felt so bad he really got sick. It always bothered Andy to see the poor old hound look so forlorn. He knew what it was like, to be lonesome. The best treatment was to take him hunting, but sometimes just a little respectful conversation used to help. He wondered if he hadn't sounded respectful enough to this old fellow just now.

As agreeably as he could Andy remarked, "The truth is, sir, I've just got a bit woozy from the altitude. You reckon I'll get used to it?"

"Sure, skipper, everybody does." The old man sat slumped and woeful. "Catarrh's somethin' else again. She grabs aholt of you and you're ruint. Here I am, only seventy-two years old, and ready for the grave before my time. Not that anybody gives a good doggone."

"Where does your catarrh bother you?" Andy asked politely.

"All over, all over. Got it in my joints—hipbones and elbows. Even got it in my skin. My hair's fallin' out. Oh, it's a cruel world, skipper."

Andy was thinking how the one sure way he had always been able to bring the old hound out of his sorrows was to act even more misfortunate. He used to put his head in his hands and pretend to moan and groan, and pretty soon the dog would be licking his hands and wagging that long, sad tail. By trying to cheer Andy up he just naturally had to feel better himself. Andy wondered if it would work now.

Gloomily he said, "Yes, sir, it's a *mortal* cruel world. I been wishing I never got born, myself. Been sleeping out on the hard ground, got nothing to eat. I think I'm starving to death, and just as well if I do."

The old man looked at him—Andy thought he seemed to brighten a little. "That a fact? You got no home? No folks?"

"I've got a father and an uncle, but they're starving, too." It wasn't even very hard to sound mournful. "And my grandpa's gone to the Veterans' Home. I'll never see him again."

"HAH!" yelled the old man so loudly that Andy jumped. "That's what they tried to do to me! My own children, too, but I met 'em at the front door with my bird gun. Told 'em, by cootie, they wasn't going to lock me up in a old-folks' home. I got a lot of life left in me yet!" His white mustache puffed out fiercely with every word.

Andy decided the catarrh must have eased off somewhat. He certainly wished he understood people as well as he did animals.

"Come on, skipper," the old man was saying, "I'll buy you a beefsteak so's you don't cave in. You look puny."

Andy protested, but the aged blue eyes began to look wounded again. And the fact was, during the last few days he had eaten so little he really did feel somewhat narrow. As they elbowed up together at the counter of a hash house his mouth began to water. Every miner in the place was eating steak. The plump women who cooked and served were joking with the men—the place was alive with laughter. A billowy pink girl approached them.

"Howdy, Misery, what'll it be? The usual?"

"Double order. I got a friend with me." The old man spoke with such pride, it was as if he must have been lonely a long, long time. "See 'em, skipper." He glanced down the length of the counter. "All these boys, bellerin' to each other, think they're doing fine, got friends galore? Ten years ago it was me—full of grits and on top of the world. When this camp was young I was rich. Or thought I was."

Andy began to feel uneasy. If the old man was really poor now—and his clothes were shabby enough—he shouldn't be buying steaks. "Listen, sir," he began, "I'd just as soon have flapjacks—"

"No such! Not when you eat with Misery Jones. Oh, you think I can't pay the tab maybe." That made the old man let out a gusty laugh. "I got money, skipper. Plenty of it. That ain't what I meant by 'rich.' In the old days I had other things. This town was mine. Everybody was my friend. All gone now—drifted off, run off, died off. I had a family, then, too—sons—"

When his voice faded Andy prompted him. "Yes, sir, you had sons?"

"No good, skipper. Gave 'em my mine to run, and they tried to steal it from me. Thought they'd put me away in a safe place and take all the profit. Well, it's all over now. The mine's sold—I gave 'em their share and

44

told 'em to git. It's a fearful hard thing for a father to face up to—knowin' his boys are no good. What'd I say, skipper? You look like a shadow just passed over your grave. Here now, you're probably hungry. Heave to and eat."

The steaks had been set sizzling before them. At the sight and smell even Andy's troubles got swamped in a surge of hunger. Forgetting most of Grandma's instructions on table manners, he seized the knife and fork and went at it. He had the steak half gobbled before he realized the old man wasn't eating much. He was watching.

"You really was starved," Misery marveled. "I thought maybe that was a small fib, tryin' to work me for a free meal. Go ahead, boy, it does me good to see somebody have all that appetite."

"This is doing me good, too," Andy assured him fervently. "Thank you, sir."

The old man's eyes were thoughtful. "You say you got no roof over you, neither? Well, then, come along home. I got a big place, empty as me. Come along and bring your relatives—if I don't like 'em I'll shout at 'em, but that's better than echoes. I swear, if I got to stay there alone many more days, listenin' to them echoes, I'm done for."

Andy knew, of course, that it was a preposterous idea. He knew he should refuse politely and take his leave and get on about the business of finding some gold. Then he saw the liveliness begin to go out of the old

45

man. Absently Misery reached for his bottle of pills. And in spite of his better judgment Andy began to nod.

"If the others are willing—we'll come."

It was a big old house, shaggy and weatherbeaten as its owner. But it had once been elegant. The porch was framed in carved latticework and the front door was very genteel, with an oval glass window. Pausing at the gate, Brett stood looking up at it silently. Hep clapped Andy across the shoulders.

"A splendid abode, nephew, splendid!"

"Too splendid." Brett glanced down at Andy sternly. "You remember my telling you not to take up with strangers? You've been made a fool of, somehow. Nobody offers free lodgings in a good solid house like that." He started to turn away. Andy followed, disheartened. He certainly wasn't going to try to explain how it was with a lonely old hound.

Hep protested. "Aren't you being a mite hasty, Billy? The lad may have some game of his own—he's clever enough, I'll wager."

And then the door of the house opened and Misery himself came down the steps—a proud figure, his pale hair uncovered and his old shoulders erect.

"Come on in, gents," he called. "You may think the boy's foolin', but he ain't. I'd be obliged to have you for company—you can see the place is big as a barn. Unless maybe it ain't fine enough for you. I know it needs paint—"

Brett shook his head. "It's a good house, no need to

46

belittle it. But I never took charity yet. Where I stay, I pay—and just now I'm not able."

"You sound like a stubborn cuss," the old man observed amiably. "You want to pay, then do it—whenever you can. I won't take much, though. I got my own brand of stubbornness. Goes agin my grain, to take pay for somethin' I got too much of."

Brett still looked uncertain. He and the old man eyed each other a long minute.

Hep put in anxiously, "For the love of our aching bones, Billy, let's not look a gift horse in the mouth. I'd just as soon not sleep on bedrock again tonight."

Andy saw his father flick a glance his way, then reluctantly he faced Misery Jones again. "A good bed would do us all good. But before I accept your hospitality you've got to know this: You've invited a hardluck outfit into your home. My name's Will Brett. I'm on the outs with the law up north. I have no job and I'm not likely to find one soon. The sheriff of Black Hawk has already been at work—he's called the district and spread the bad word about me. I was turned down by six mines today; no reason to suppose that tomorrow will be better. Maybe you'd like to think twice about us."

The old man seemed to grow a few inches taller as Brett spoke. "Son, if you got hard times you've come to the right place—couldn't find a better spot to be misfortunate in. They don't call me 'Misery' for nothin'. Drag what's left of you on inside—there's beans on the stove."

Seven

"Are you sure it was Duke who warned off the bosses?"
Hep asked, as he and Brett talked together in low voices
next morning. Andy, lying abed in the small room ad-
joining theirs, stretched his ears to listen.

"One of the mine owners told me outright," his father
said angrily. "The Association had a call from Duke
three or four days ago. He must've figured we'd head
for the richest camp around. Why doesn't that buzzard
get off my back?"

"What's this Association thing?"

"The Mine Owners' Association. All the operators
belong—so they've all got the word."

"I don't see it," Hep complained. "What's it to them
—what happened in a card game up in Black Hawk?"

"Oh, Duke's too smart to let it go at that. Told them
all about the matter up in Central City, then clinched it

by telling them I was a well-known high-grader. That put them off me for good. One fellow almost threw me out bodily." Suddenly curious, he asked, "How was it you didn't get the same treatment when you applied for work?"

Uncle Hep coughed and fussed and took so long answering that Brett went on irritably. "You didn't look for a job, did you?"

"Now, Billy! You know I'm no pick-and-shovel man!"

"You've set off plenty of black powder. I don't know anyone handier with dynamite. But no matter—the mines are closed to us, thanks to Duke. The point is, we must make some money one way or another. Here's my thought—" His voice dropped so low that Andy couldn't hear.

All at once Hep burst out, genuinely shocked, "No! No, Billy! Not that! You're my older brother, and I've gone along with you on most things, but this I won't—"

There was some more quiet mutter, then Hep said flatly, "The only time I ever want to see the inside of a bank is when I make a deposit there. No use to argue—" He stamped across the room and went out; Andy heard the door shut hard.

Slipping out of bed, he dressed quietly. He could hear his father moving around in there—the first time he had been alone. Andy tried to stiffen up his belly against the nervous feeling, because he was going to walk on in and have a talk. Right now.

When he opened the door, he saw his father start, and make a move as if to hide what he was doing. But not soon enough—Andy had already seen that he was cleaning a gun.

"Don't you knock before you come into a room?" Brett asked, but the tone wasn't so biting this morning. He went on with the business of the gun intently, as if he had come to some kind of decision during the night.

"I'm sorry. I forgot." Andy sat down on a chair nearby. "I wanted to talk to you."

"Then do it."

"I know I'm a bother"—Andy had rehearsed this, and in spite of his father's short shake of the head, he rushed on—"but I don't aim to be a burden. I used to help out around the store. And I worked for the farmer down the road every afternoon after school. You just tell me what I should do and I'll do it."

"I've already told you." His father was polishing the barrel of the pistol, a gleaming, wicked little black revolver hardly any bigger than his hand. "Told you to stay clear of strangers, yet you go out and take up with one. You don't pay much mind to what I say. Not that I blame you—I don't know why you should have any special respect for me."

"Well, I do!" Andy denied. "I mean, I didn't think it was wrong. Misery started talking to me—"

"He's all right. But the next man could be a killer. Or a thief. You could wake up to find his hand in your pocket and his knife at your throat."

Andy said wryly, "He wouldn't get much out of me. Somebody already stole my nine dollars."

His father glanced over keenly. "How did that happen?"

"I don't know. I guess I shouldn't have left it in the knapsack." He tried not to sound pointed.

"That's too bad." Brett slid the gun into a leather holster that was strapped to his side under his arm. "You seem to have inherited the family tendency toward mishap. But it does no good to groan over yesterday's bad luck. Maybe sooner or later I can replace your loss. At least I aim to show you I can pay for the roof over our heads."

There was a fierceness about the quiet words that made Andy realize how deep it cut across the grain for his father to be penniless. It helped him forgive the matter of the knapsack. And after all, he said he was intending to pay it back.

"I don't mind—" he began.

"Well, I do," Brett cut in curtly. "Your grandfather may have told you a lot of things about me, but never that I was a deadbeat."

"Grandpa?" Andy was astounded. "He never said anything about you at all! When I asked him, he always said he didn't know."

For an instant Brett's poker face slipped; he looked surprised. "He never prepared you for—any of this?"

"Did he know all about you?" Andy asked wonderingly.

"All? He knew enough. Enough to lay down the rules of the game: He'd raise you properly and decently, but I'd have to stay out of it. He always thought I wasn't good enough for your mother—and he was right. She was a fine, delicate, gentle lady, as far above me as an angel. If she'd lived, things would have been different. I'd have gone on working the claim we had in Central City—I might have proved myself to him. But that's past. Without her, I didn't much care what I did. I just knew that as far as you were concerned, your grandparents would bring you up well. That's why I went along with the bargain."

"And that's why you never came to see me."

"I suppose they didn't tell you the whole story because they wanted you to make up your own mind someday." Brett kept flipping a penny, over and over, restlessly. "Your grandfather is a very fair man. He was hoping I'd make something of myself, I guess. If I'd known that—" Brett shrugged. "But 'if' is a loser's word. I'm through losing. And done with gambling. After today things are going to be different."

"Yes, sir," Andy agreed impulsively. "Maybe we'll get lucky. I'm usually pretty lucky myself. I'll bet we find some gold."

His father seemed faintly amused. "Never gamble on a thing unless you know the odds are in your favor. There are surer ways to make a dollar than looking for gold." He stood up and put on his coat. The gun didn't show at all, even as a bulge under his arm.

"What are you going to do, if you can't get a job?" Andy asked.

"Don't question me, boy." He seemed to retreat into that defensive, stony-faced stranger again. As he picked up the black hat, he seemed to remember something. "By the way, your hat reminds me of your esteemed grandfather. Since you've come into a new life you may want to look around for a new one. And by tonight I'd say we'll be able to pay for it."

It turned into a bad day. Rain drummed against the weathered boards of the house and coursed down the windowpanes. In the kitchen a good fire in the wood range made a close, friendly, crackling to be sat around. Uncle Hep had developed a blister on his heel—said he thought he'd let the job hunting go for a day. Old Misery was glad enough for the company, and the two of them leaned back in their chairs and put their feet up on the woodbox as they talked along about a thousand subjects. It was almost like being back in Grandpa's store again, but Andy didn't feel at ease for some reason. Something was making him strangely nervous. Roaming the room, he came to stand at the window, trying to look out past the streaming rain water, while the talk went on behind him.

"Yep, Misery's been my nickname all m' life, ever since I was a young sprout and fell in a glory hole and broke m' leg. For a long time my luck wasn't real bad, but the last few years it's been a she-devil."

And then Hep was going on about their own troubles. "This fellow, Duke Dade . . . sheriff up north . . . slick as a peeled snake. Had it in for Billy a long time now, spreading lies . . . told the Association he's a high-grader."

Restlessly Andy wandered back to the stove. "What's a high-grader, Uncle Hep?"

Misery answered first. "That's a feller who indulges in the skulduggerous thievery of picture-rock, skipper."

It didn't mean a thing to Andy.

Uncle Hep explained. "Picture-rock is the prettiest sight in the world, nephew—the pure, sweet gold out of the heart of a vein. Many's the mine owner who never sees the half of his best high-grade ore, on account of the natural eagerness of his faithful employees to carry it home with them in their lunch buckets or pants pockets."

"Or hid in other places," Misery added. "When I was runnin' my mine, I had to fire a feller with a sweet tooth for the stuff. He used to carry it out in his jaw. And all along I was thinkin' he chawed tobacco." Then he fixed Hep with a sober look. "That's one kind of mischief I don't hold with. Hope them reports from your sheriff was just rumors."

"Not even that," Hep told him quickly. "Pure lies. Billy not only wouldn't high-grade, but so far he's never had the chance. He and I owned a claim up in Central City and worked it together. And he's done enough prospecting that he swings a pretty good pick. But he's never been employed to break another man's rock. That's why I'd like to flatten that scoundrel, Duke, for spreading such tales."

"Sheriffs ain't all they might be sometimes." Misery nodded. "I remember up in Virginia City, back in the sixties . . ." He drifted off into a long story about a sheriff who had turned out to be the secret leader of the very gang he was supposed to be trying to catch. Most times it would have interested Andy, but he kept feeling the tension pull tighter inside him as the minutes ticked off on the brass clock above the stove.

By afternoon he was ready to explode. The two men were still swapping that aimless talk; the rain still gusted against the window. When it finally let up a little, Andy lost no time in getting out of the house. The streets were a muddy slop. Drayage wagons, even light buckboards, slithered in the deep ruts and horses plunged to get their footing. Yet the rushing life of Victor hadn't slackened. On the hillside above town ore trains moved, their cars piled high with rock. And over each shaft the big wheels spun atop their gaunt scaffolding. They had an ominous name for that tall structure that rose above each mine— it was called a "gallows frame." For some reason the thought turned Andy to wondering about his father, and he shivered.

It was as he walked along a side street that he saw the sign: "Madame Fortuna—Knows All. *Ask any question. Ten Cents.*" Roughly lettered on a piece of cardboard, it was tacked to the door of a basement. The dwelling above looked ready to cave in—a jerry-built clapboard house with large patches of tar paper covering broken windows. The roof was sagging and the steps up to the porch were coming loose. The ones down to the little door under the porch were dug out of raw earth— the rain had left them slippery. Andy picked his way down. For a minute he stood in the drizzle, hesitant.

He didn't dare ask the question that was really uppermost in his mind, but there was another almost as important. He wondered if this were really a good fortuneteller—then decided to risk it. Digging down into his Levis, he found his money. Ever since he had lost most of his savings he had carried the four dimes in his pocket. With only the least qualm of fear he knocked.

Someone must have been waiting very near. Almost at once the door opened a crack and a piece of wrapping paper was thrust out. A low, ghostly voice said, "Write question, please."

Fortunately Andy had a stub of pencil in his pocket. Printing carefully, he wrote: *What does my father think of me?* When the door opened again he shoved the paper back through the crack and followed it with the dime, which was taken from him by warm feminine fingers. It seemed a long wait—for some reason he sensed that the person on the other side of the door was laughing, though he heard no sound. At last the hinges creaked and the paper was returned—the door shut quickly as Andy read his answer:

Dirty, Lazy, Worthless, Imbecile Boy.

Slowly he started to mount the stairs, the paper

crumpled in his hand. This must be a pretty makeshift gypsy, he thought, to give out a rude fortune like that. He was chagrined to have been rooked out of a dime. And then he looked up to see a man standing above him —a young man whose light yellow hair seemed to bristle in anger.

"She's at it again!" he shouted as he ran down the steps past Andy. "Wait, young sir, you shall have your money back!" Bursting through the doorway, he seized someone inside. "You little witch, have I not told you . . . ?" And then as the door swung wider Andy saw who his "gypsy" was—a girl slightly younger than himself, tousled, skinny, blond-haired as the young man was. She began to gabble in some foreign language—it was startling to hear her babble it out in that high, childish voice. She kept saying something that sounded to Andy like "Shay fan, shay fan!"

The man shook his head and answered sharply in the same tongue. When he began to shake her, Andy snatched at his sleeve.

"Don't, please, sir. She didn't mean any harm."

"She—must—give back—this money—" The young man spoke between clenched teeth.

Tearfully the little girl threw a dime in Andy's direction. "It is not fair," she cried in English. "I gave him a true fortune. I said he was lazy—he isn't working, is he? And dirty—you can see that. And an imbecile, because he believes in fortunetellers!" She broke away and ran into the gloom of the basement.

The young man tore the sign from the door and

stepped inside. Icily he said, "I apologize, sir. You have your money. Good day."

Andy went. But the business had upset him. Unhappily he looked down at himself. Never thought much about whether he was dirty or not—it didn't seem important. But it actually had been a couple of weeks since he'd had a bath—might even be the reason for some of his father's coolness toward him. He'd evidently been irritated by the tattered old hat. Fingering the dime, Andy considered going home, but it was a matter he would just as soon not bring up with Misery Jones and Uncle Hep. With some regrets he decided he had better invest a little money in privacy and turned in at the first barbershop.

The tub was in a cubbyhole at the back of the shop. As he eased down into it, Andy had to admit the hot water felt good. Leaning back, he soaked luxuriously. The barber and his customer were paying him no attention—he could just see them through the open door. They were talking about business and how the district was growing.

"Now this is the kind of thing we've got to put an end to, if we ever want respectable folks to move here." The barber picked up a copy of the evening paper and handed it to the man in the chair. "Just look at that. Right in broad daylight this morning this masked man walks in, pulls a gun—"

Andy looked up sharply, and his heart turned over. For even at that distance he could read the black headlines: BANDIT ROBS CRIPPLE CREEK BANK!

Eight

The more Andy thought about it the madder he got and the faster he walked. He wasn't being reasonable any more or searching for excuses. The facts were too suspicious to be argued away. It kept making a sick surge of shame inside him, and to overcome it, he had to be mad. Good and mad. It must have showed, too, for as he came up onto the front porch of the house Hep roused in the hammock where he was stretched out.

"What's up, nephew? You come to grief?"

"No, sir."

"Can't fool your old uncle. Did you get robbed again or something?"

It was almost the truth—he did feel robbed, of all the wonderful hopes he'd had. Of the dream of someday belonging to somebody, being proud of somebody.

"Drat it," Hep was shaking his head, "I've been afraid you might get hurt around this confounded town. A mining camp is no place for a boy and your father ought to know that."

In a rush Andy tried to cover up his wound, casting about for any kind of answer. "I'm just—upset. I got into a fight with some people today, some foreigners. They talked a lingo I couldn't understand." He was making conversation feverishly now, because within the depths of the house he could hear his father talking.

"Ah, yes," Uncle Hep was going on, "there've been a number of misguided Europeans come to this country looking for those legendary streets paved with gold. What was the fight about?"

"I'm not sure," Andy hedged. "They kept saying 'naw, naw, naw' and 'wee, wee, wee' at each other."

"Sounds like French." Hep smiled expansively. "Takes me back to my undergraduate days, though I regret to say I did poorly in that particular study."

"You went to college?" Andy was genuinely impressed. He'd never met anyone who had. "Then do you know what it means to say 'Shay fan, shay fan'?" He sort of swallowed the last syllable, the same way the little girl had.

"*J'ai faim?* Oh, yes, I well remember that lesson—a most important phrase to learn. It means 'I'm hungry.'"

Andy was startled. This would have to be thought about some more. Just now, though, he heard his father coming.

"Did he go to college, too?" he asked with a glance toward the house.

60

"Billy? No, he ran off from home instead. I still recall that farewell letter—he made a delightful pun. Said one doesn't need a sheepskin when one is already a black sheep. Oh, he was a great one for getting in scrapes, even in those— Well, brother, good evening."

Brett stood in the doorway surveying them. To Andy he nodded. "I've been waiting to see you. Did you go shopping, as I suggested?" It was said in polite, almost friendly, tones. As he held the door for Andy to step inside, it was evident that he was more content with himself than usual. He led the way into the next room where they couldn't be overheard. When he turned, he had pulled a roll of banknotes from his pocket.

"What kind of hat did you find?" he asked as he peeled a ten-dollar bill from the roll.

Defiantly Andy answered, "I reckon this one's good enough for me."

His father eyed him more sharply. "What's happened to you? You're looking crisper tonight—not so woolly and worried. That's a good sign. I like a boy who speaks up firm. Keep the hat if you like it. But you'll need a change of clothes—"

"I washed up today." Andy was particularly sore about having gone to all that trouble. "I reckon I'm as clean as—anybody else."

"You do look well scrubbed." His father studied him even more closely, as if perplexed. "Better and better. But, as I say, you'll be needing some spending money—" He extended the ten-dollar bill with a slight flourish.

"I won't take it." Andy drew back.

"How's that?" Brett stared as if he'd been slapped. "What do you mean?"

"I don't want your dirty money!" Andy yelled. "I don't care whether you like me or not. I don't care about anything! I don't care—I don't care—!"

He had backed up against the wall, half expecting his father to seize him and whip him. Instead, Brett stood rigid, the expression fading out of his face, leaving it like candle wax. Slowly his hand clenched, crumpling the bill, and in his eyes was a look of defeat—yes, of guilt. Andy turned and ran.

It was starting to rain again as he pounded down the front steps and kicked open the gate. He was distantly aware that Uncle Hep was calling after him, asking what the matter was. But he didn't stop.

Darkness was settling early upon the town, and as it deepened Andy was part of it. He felt shadowy inside as he drifted along the nearly deserted streets. He had no identity—he could have been invisible for all anyone cared. There in the houses, in the lighted windows, people were eating supper—gathered together with their families, talking warmly. Shut off from this chilly, wet, lonesome, outside world. In times past he had never minded being by himself, but then he'd had his imaginings to fall back on. He had built pictures about himself. Someday . . . someday. . . . And now it was the day after someday.

Under his feet the earth seemed to vibrate as if it

were turning on giant machinery. He knew the sound must come from one of the buildings nearby—he remembered vaguely being aware of it before, though the noise of traffic and trains had drowned it out. Now with everyone inside at dinner he could sense it, huge wheels grinding like a pulse—a heartless mechanical kind of pulse, keeping alive this world of strange people.

Painfully he longed for the quiet of wheat fields where the summer rain fell softly. Of barns, warm and silent except for the breathing of cattle. He clenched up inside whenever he thought of his animals. The raccoon, the old dog—even the scratchy little yellow cat—

And for some reason he thought of the French girl. *I'm hungry.* Every time a kitty meowed, you could be sure it was for food. A hungry one quivers clear out to the tip of its lofty little tail. Even though he didn't much like cats, he never could resist giving them milk. Now more than ever he could sympathize with the pang of an empty belly and the misery of being badgered. His steps took on new direction.

In the darkness it was hard to find the street again, and when he did come to the house he saw no light in the basement rooms. One showed above, however, shining from the few windowpanes that were left. Andy had started to go up to the front door when a movement caught his eye—something lighter than the shadows was crouched below, far back in the doorway under the stairs. Feeling in his pocket, he found a match—always carried such things for emergencies, as Uncle Hep put it. Shielding it from the rain with his cupped hand, he scraped it with his thumbnail and the flame flared up.

She was down there—wet and bedraggled, clutching a thin coat about her, the tawny hair plastered to her face. With wide, dark eyes she looked up at him, ready to scratch.

"Howdy," he said carelessly, coming down off the porch. Keeping a safe distance, he got out a dime and held it up. "I came to pay you for"—the match went out—"for my fortune. It was good advice. You earned this." He tried to keep any teasing out of his voice. In the pitch-black he couldn't see her, but he heard her move. Out of the darkness a quick hand found his and extracted the dime with fierce urgency.

"In fact"—he scrummaged in his pocket again—"I think it was worth twice the price. I did need a bath, all right. Here—"

She came closer to take the second dime. In the faint glow from the window above he could see that she was smiling tensely. "You are a gentleman. I am sorry I said you were worthless. *Sacré bleu*, you are rich! Do you have enough money to buy a gold mine? I'll sell you a good one. Very cheap."

Andy thought she must be actually quite hungry, to try a whopper like that. "I'm sorry," he said tolerantly, "but I can't afford a gold mine right now. Why do you need money if you've got gold?"

"Because the gold is in the ground, *stupide*, and my brother, Remi, is a very bad miner. He knows nothing about it. He spends everything for these ugly motors and the awful dynamite, so he cannot hire men to dig the gold, and so we do not eat. He is a beast—he told me we would be rich. Hah! we will not live long enough." Her talk was scornful but her lips were trembling. "Please, I will sell you this mine for a hundred dollars."

"I don't think your brother would like that," Andy said, half amused.

"Ah, you do not believe me! Men—they are all alike. Remi, he will not listen either. So stubborn, like a mule he is! He has been trying to keep the mine in spite of all. Now it is too late, too late. How I hate him! Oh, I am so cold!"

"You'd better go inside," Andy advised. She really was shivering hard.

"I cannot go in because the door is locked. We cannot pay the rent," she said furiously. "So now he will have to sell. The fool, he is up there in the house now, bargaining with them over this rathole of a cellar. He thinks he can sell them only part of the mine. Why should they settle for part? They know we have had nothing but beans to eat for weeks. Awful, awful beans! They will take it all—he won't get a hundred dollars for it."

To Andy it was beginning to sound like the truth. And if so, there was no time to waste. No time to think it through. Impulsively he said, "Don't let him do it! I told you, I can't buy your mine, but my father—he's in need of work right now. And there's an old man at home who has some money. Why don't you and your brother come along with me? Maybe they'd be interested."

She didn't wait for more. Turning, she called shrilly, "Remi! Remi! We are saved! Come out here quickly!" Running up the steps onto the porch, she began to bang on the door.

Left below in the dark, Andy suffered some second thoughts. It had been a rash thing to suggest and he wasn't even sure why he had done it. To help these people he didn't know? Or for his father's sake—for his own sake, so that the foolish, long-ago hope could stay alive a little longer? It was a crazy notion, but—for better or for worse—he was going to give his father one more chance.

Nine

Andy had never known any mules personally. But he had been acquainted with a horse—a young buckskin that had belonged to a farm just down the road from Grandpa's place. A spirited animal, it stepped out proudly when there was a smart saddle on its back, but it detested a plow. Somehow this fellow, Remi, had the same air.

A handsome young man with a large, noble nose and that wind-blown forelock of light hair, he held himself proudly, as if he were doing them a slight favor to have dinner in Misery Jones' kitchen. The old man didn't seem to notice; he was too tickled to have all that crowd around.

"Hope y'all don't mind if it's plain miner's strawberries for supper," he said over his shoulder, stirring the pot on the stove.

"Strawberries?" trilled the little girl—her name was Josephine but she had already invited Andy to call her Josey. "Strawberries! How delicious." The way she said it sounded more like "day-lee-shoes." To Remi she said a whole sentence in French, but he stopped her.

"It is not polite to speak so that everyone cannot understand." Turning back to the men, he went on talking of his mine. "I bought the lease some months ago from the man who first staked the claim. He put down a shaft, but had no money for equipment. I myself did not realize it would be so costly. It has taken most of my capital, so"—he shrugged—"I have none left to hire men to dig."

"How deep is your shaft?" Uncle Hep asked judiciously.

"Four hundred feet. Three crosscuts are begun."

"How many drifts?"

Remi frowned slightly. "I—do not know this 'drifts.' "

"That's your side tunnels off the main crosscut." Misery came over to join them, bringing the heavy iron pot all a-steam. "Here we go. Everybody dive in."

As he set it in the middle of the table, Josey swallowed hard, staring at the big muddy stew of red kidney beans as if it were poison. "This is the strawberry of the miner?" she said with a sickly smile. "What a nice little joke."

Andy could almost sympathize with her; he was getting tired of beans himself. It seemed to be all that Misery knew how to cook. The other men were none too enthusiastic, either, though Misery was spooning the stuff onto his plate with zest.

"Where's your claim located at, buster?" he asked.

Remi winced at the term of address. "It is to the west of here, sir—up on the Squaw Mountain."

"Squaw ain't a bad location. Pay-rock runs all through there. What's the name of your works? Mebbe I know it."

"It is filed as the *Sidewinder*." Remi spoke the name with displeasure. "I am told it is a kind of deadly snake. I have tried to have it changed, but this becomes difficult."

"Don't see nothin' wrong with the name, m'self." Misery looked around at the others with a gleam of excitement in his eyes. "Sidewinder's a little feller, don't look like much, don't seem to be makin' much progress movin' sideways, until all of a sudden—zingo! He strikes! Faster'n lightnin'. Could be the same with your gold, buster. Why, I'd near consider buyin' into the deal just because that name sounds like luck."

It was plain to see that the old man's easygoing manners had offended Remi. Like the young horse, you couldn't just slap a saddle on his back roughly.

"I have not yet decided whether I will sell—" he began loftily.

"What?" Josey cried aghast, her thin face alive with shock. "What is this you are saying? Where do we sleep tonight, then, eh?"

Remi reddened with embarrassment. Glancing around

the table, harassed, his eye met Will Brett's. "You, sir —you have not asked me a host of questions. What is your position?"

Brett was flipping a penny—up and over. In a wry, quiet voice he said, "Just that of a man who needs work. If it's labor you lack, I can swing a singlejack as well as the next. And my brother, here, is an expert at setting off black powder."

"As fer just plain know-how," Misery put in brightly, "I been lookin' at rock, good and bad, for thirty-five years."

But strangely Remi still turned to Brett when he spoke. "No man works free."

Brett tossed the penny again. "The time can come to anyone when it's to his advantage to pool his resources with another's for possible mutual benefit."

Josey looked to Andy, as if baffled by the slow twist of the language. He was a little surprised himself at how his father's words had soothed Remi's nerves. The Frenchman was smiling now—they were all being polite, talking about going out to look at the mine tomorrow. Misery said he'd find some sheets for a couple more beds upstairs.

With a deep breath of satisfaction, the little French girl attacked her supper. Andy heard her vow under her breath, "And perhaps soon we shall have no more abominable beans, I think."

That next day, as Andy stood with the others around the gaping hole in the ground, he got a strange prickly

70

feeling at the back of his neck. For some reason he could feel his luck rising, as it never had before. Something about that raw shaft, the stark gallows frame towering over it, the wheel and its cable falling away into the darkness below—it made him shiver with expectancy. The other end of the cable slanted down to a small shed nearby where it was attached to a drum powered by a shiny new gasoline motor.

Misery was eying the machine skeptically. "Them dang things is expensive to run. Steam's cheaper—but that'll come later. We'll put in a boiler when we expand operations."

Andy could see the Frenchman bridle again at the way the old man took things for granted. "I believe I shall use electricity eventually," Remi remarked coolly.

"We'll see." Misery roamed over to the dump. Hep was already there, picking through the rock. "Granite." The old man hefted a piece in his hand. "Red granite. Not so good. I'd ruther see a little quartz."

"This claim is leased from the old mine over there." Remi motioned toward a rusting shaft house that rose just beyond the curve of the hill. "It is finished now, but in its day that one was rich. The assayer assures me that my ore is promising, too."

"Assayers are a bunch of crooks," Misery informed him. "They'll fence for high-graders and run false reports for smelters. Fact is, they'll do most anything wicked. Wouldn't put it past one of 'em to help some slicker sell you a salted mine."

The Frenchman drew himself up. "Salt? I believe I

would know salt if I see it."

"Oh, jumpin' jackhammers," the old man groaned. "You think I mean table salt? That's the trouble, too many amateurs messin' up the district, don't know gold from a pyrite."

Remi turned away muttering, ". . . uneducated old buffoon."

But Hep was agreeing with Misery. "I'm afraid granite's a poor bet when you're looking for gold. This district is one of the few places on earth where it's ever been known to occur, I believe—"

Andy was watching his father. Brett had roamed off up the hillside above the shaft. For quite a while he had been wandering about up there, aimlessly picking through the grass. Now he came slowly back down to join them.

"Prospects don't appear too bright, Billy," Hep was saying. "I'd say we'd be wasting our time."

"Can't judge a deck by the top card," Brett remarked. "Shall we go below and have a look?" He seemed his usual expressionless self, but Andy was beginning to be able to detect small signs in that careful face. Now he saw a glint in the dark eyes, subtle as heat lightning in a thunderhead. His father had seen something up there on the hillside.

"I think these gentlemen feel it is useless," Remi said icily, "but you, sir, if you wish to go down I shall be happy to operate the skip." He set about starting the gasoline motor. As soon as it was humming evenly he threw a lever and the wheel above the shaft began to turn. Up came a cage—an iron framework without sidewalls, just a plank floor. It didn't look very sound to Andy, but his father was beckoning the other two men onto it. To Andy he shook his head.

"You stay up here. A mine is no place for kids."

As Remi shifted gears the cage dropped out of sight into the hole; cable began to pay out rapidly. Andy almost forgot his own disappointment as he stared at it —racing, faster and faster—and then the Frenchman applied the brake, it slowed and came to a stop. Andy let out his breath in a sigh of relief.

"Don't worry. Remi is good with these motors. It is all he knows." Josey was grinning up at him sidewise. " 'Kid'—your father called you a young goat. I think this is amusing!" She dug her fingers into his side, then danced off before he could get back at her. Going to stand near her brother, she advised him impudently, "Don't let the old one bother you. He is rich, maybe he will buy this horrid mine. You will sell! You must!"

"Be quiet," he told her, but he looked dejected.

Andy felt he should try to explain one thing, or the whole business might fall through. "Misery doesn't mean to be so bossy, sir, but he's pretty old, and he's been all alone for a long time. Underneath he's sad—he takes a lot of pills."

Remi nodded as if he partly understood. "This is a strange country. Beautiful and rich. But the people— they are without heart."

Andy could agree with that—it had certainly been heartless of his father not to let him go below. Of course, there was still an awkwardness between them, left over from that bad moment the evening before. Andy felt terrible about that. Now that he was calmer he was ready to admit that he had no proof—none at all—that his father had done a thing wrong. Even the Constitution of the United States said that a man is innocent until proven guilty. He had practically broken the Constitution—judging his father that way.

At last a bell rang three times from somewhere below and Remi threw the switch again to bring the cage up. When it rose into view, it was plain to see that at least two of the three men were pleased. Hep looked unhappy, but Brett seemed satisfied, and Misery was beaming outright.

"Not too bad, she's not too bad. Streak of sylvanite down there—low grade, but we could scratch enough out of her to pay for more powder and timber."

Remi was looking to Brett, as if his word were the deciding one.

He nodded. "We're willing to risk our time and effort if you would care to go shares."

"But I've got to boss the job below," Misery put in. "I can smell gold like it was perfume. Gimme the go-ahead and I'll show you where to cut your drifts. I'll even grubstake the lot of ye while we're tryin' to make it pay off."

Brett went on. "I'm sure we could arrive at an agreement on a fair division of profits, after expenses are paid and Misery reimbursed for our room and board. There wouldn't be much to split at first, but where there's low-grade ore there may be pockets of smelter grade. We could extend the works fairly rapidly with three of us down the shaft, and you, sir, attending matters aboveground. That is, if you approve such an arrangement."

For the first time the Frenchman seemed to take spirit. "That is good. I need the time—to manage. I shall run the machinery, keep the books—"

"What can I do?" Andy burst out, unable to keep still any longer. "There must be some kind of job for me."

His father looked at him thoughtfully but before he could answer, Josey spoke up sweetly. "Andrew will aid me in the home, that is what he will do. He will chop the wood for the stove. And I"—she took a deep breath and went on dreamily—"I shall cook!"

PART II
PICTURE-ROCK

Ten

Behind the shed and shaft the mountain slid away upward in a long, rolling slope, crested with summer sky. The hillside was studded with little piles of rock where men had dug their small glory holes and gone away disappointed. Those deserted mounds were lonesome as gravestones—they probably marked the end of a lot of hopes, Andy thought.

And yet he was drawn to this place for some reason. It was quiet—not the peaceful quiet of the fields, but a whisperous, promising stillness that filled him with imaginings. Even the old buildings of the abandoned mine, rising from just beyond the profile of the hill, seemed to give off muted echoes of past riches rumbling down its chutes. Around him was a sort of humming— of bees among the high-mountain flowers, of the earth warming itself under the afternoon sun. Or was it the turning of his own inner wheels?

He sat on one of the piles of rock contemplating the little works below. The *Sidewinder's* unpainted shed looked small and shabby. No chutes rose behind the shaft, no railroad sidings laced the ground around. What ore they had dug this past week had been brought up in the bucket, then loaded onto a mule-drawn wagon. Remi had hired a freighter to come every day and haul their rock to the mill. After the teamster had collected his fee, there wasn't much left to show for all their work. Uncle Hep had come right out and said they were wasting their time, doing business on such a small scale. But the others were full of hopes. Whether or not it was common sense, they seemed to share this buzzing excitement that Andy felt as he sat and looked at their mine.

Down there in the shed, Remi practically hovered over the account book, copying the cost figures and the meager profits in his delicate, spidery script as elegantly as if he were lettering out a birth certificate. And old Misery, in his hard-boiled hat, was up at daybreak every morning—couldn't wait to get down that shaft. Even Will Brett moved with an intentness these days, spoke up more than he had at first. He had to put in a word fairly often to keep peace between Remi and the old man. But for all their squabbles, they were alive with expectations.

Looking down now, Andy felt left out. What's

worse, he knew it was at least partly his own fault for making that scene over the ten-dollar bill. His father hadn't approached him again since that night. Though he didn't seem exactly hostile, he had not even left any openings for Andy to make the first move and apologize.

Today, though, there might be a chance. Misery had knocked off early and gone home. Uncle Hep hadn't showed up yet. He always came late in the afternoon because the holes for the dynamite couldn't be drilled until the others had finished work. Everyone had to stay out of the shaft after the shot was set off—in fact, it was best to give the powder smoke all night to clear. Go back in too soon and the fumes would bring on fearful headaches. Ruin your lungs, Misery said.

Andy had learned a good deal about mining this week, just by listening to the others, but he still yearned to get down into it with both feet. He wanted to drive a pick against some rock—to look for the sheen of bright metal. He felt, more strongly than ever, that he just . . . might . . . have that "golden touch."

From down at the mine came the ringing of a bell across the stillness—three times, the signal that meant "man on the skip—hoist away." In the shack Remi left his bookkeeping and went to start the motor. Slowly Andy got to his feet and headed down the hill.

Once he paused. This was the exact spot where his father had been poking around that first morning. Andy had gone over it a hundred times since, looking for—he didn't know exactly what. Nothing here. Nothing but scrawny grass and weeds, a few chunks of red granite. He wondered if he would ever know what it was that had made his father quicken—even made him to decide to take a chance on working the mine. And a phrase came back to him, something Brett had said: Never bet unless the odds are in your favor.

As he walked on toward the mine he passed the ventilator shaft—just a hole half hidden in the brush, breathing its dank-smelling air. It was much smaller than the main shaft, just barely large enough for a man to step into it. There was a ladder down one side—it was one way to go below and explore, but somehow Andy had never been much tempted. Like crawling into a gopher hole.

The skip had reached the top now. Brett stepped off, moving stiffly as if he were bone-weary, clothes crusted with rock dust. Even his brows were shaggy with it beneath the brim of his helmet. By the time Andy reached the shed he was talking to Remi—something about needing timber. The Frenchman was putting his books in the iron safe in the corner.

"I will go to town at once, to see if I can arrange a delivery early tomorrow. Shall I lock up the shed? Your brother is not yet here—"

Brett's face tightened with irritation, but he only said, "Never mind. I'll wait for Hep a while longer. I'll lock up for you." Bending over the wash bucket, he began to sluice water over his face and arms, wincing as if the blisters on his hands smarted. He didn't notice

Andy until he'd finished toweling off. By then Remi was well along his way down the road to town and the two of them were alone.

Brett nodded a greeting. There was a trace of humor in his voice as he said, "Thought you'd be home about now, chopping wood for the little mademoiselle."

Andy answered in the same spirit. "I chopped her enough yesterday to roast a horse."

"She might try it, too," muttered his father. The unspoken truth was that Josey was the worst cook in two thousand square miles, but nobody dared mention it. "Well, somebody's got to split kindling, no matter who happens to run the kitchen." He said it almost with apology.

"I don't mind—I did it at Grandpa's. But it's no real job." Andy was fingering the pick that his father had left leaning against the side of the shed.

"You can set that inside, if you will," Brett said carelessly. "It'll have to go to the blacksmith before it can be used again."

Andy hefted it, took a two-handed grip, and brought it down hard into the earth. "I think I could handle one of these."

"Slam that into solid granite the way you just did and you'll think a mule kicked you."

Andy hurriedly set the tool inside the door of the shed. Then, turning back, he rallied his nerve. "Can't learn to do it right unless I'm taught."

Brett's straight face twitched as if he might have

smiled. "I know when a kibitzer's squirming to get into the game. You don't have to explain."

Andy hesitated, then plunged. "I'm pretty strong, sir. I used to pitch bundles all day long in summer—I worked for the farmer near us. And I dug Grandma's garden every year. I'm handy with a spade."

"You never hefted a shovel full of hardrock. That kind of work can spavin a kid before he's grown."

"I'm not a kid!" Andy broke out before he could check himself. "I mean—I'm sorry, but I'm not—not so little as all that, I mean—"

"Thunderation, I know what you mean." Brett squinted at him curiously. "What's the charm in going down into that black hole? Gold? You see all the gold I see when the rock comes up."

And fairly dull-looking ore it was, too. Greenish-gray rock without a trace of glitter about it.

"I just—want to learn how." *I want to be a partner in all this!* he pleaded silently, but he couldn't say it aloud. It wouldn't have sounded right coming from a ki—, a younger person. "I want to be able to look for gold myself someday," he finished lamely.

"The fever's got you already, eh?" His father sounded disgusted. It didn't make any sense, because they were all looking for it right now, weren't they? Andy framed the question wordlessly, wondering why people get so strange and unreasonable when they become grownups.

"So you want me to teach you the trade," Brett

mused. "My money is dirty but my skill is acceptable. Right?"

"I'm sorry I ever said that, sir," Andy told him honestly. "I was upset about—everything."

His father shrugged. "I suppose I can't blame you much. We've made a poor beginning. But our luck may have turned now. There's even a chance that the pot will turn out to be a big one. And you're partly responsible for it all. I suppose you've got the right to take a hand." He glanced toward the shaft. "I didn't want you to go below because it's dangerous down there. But then the world up here is hardly safer. I suppose the best way to avoid falling rock is to learn to duck. And that reminds me—" He turned to look at the clock inside the shed and swore under his breath. "I should tell Hep about that east wall. Where the devil is he?"

"I'll wait for him if you like," Andy offered. "I could even run the skip—"

"You could not," his father contradicted flatly. "It may look easy the way Remi does it, but one split second is the difference between a smooth ride and being piled up at the bottom of the shaft. No, we'll put the skip to bed." He started the motor and lowered the cage out of sight. "Hep can climb down the ladder in the ventilator. Anyone who's late to work deserves no favors. But I do want to leave some instructions for him." He picked up a scrap of tar paper and began to sketch a diagram on it in chalk, noting distances in feet and inches. "We're going to open a new drift—Misery worked out the plan today. I was supposed to tell Hep where to set his shot, but only the Lord knows when he will show up and I'm dogged out. So if you'll do me the favor to hang around and give this to him—" He was scribbling at the bottom of the drawing:

Tap her light—she's none too solid. And don't turn your back on the east wall.

Andy took the sheet, puzzling over the words.

"You'll learn what that means tomorrow," his father said. "Seven o'clock sharp. You take after your uncle somewhat, in your affection for gold; I hope you won't copy his tardiness."

"No, sir!" Andy tried to grasp the fact that his wish was going to be granted—he was going below. But before he could thank his father, Brett was striding off toward home.

It was nearly sundown—Andy judged it to be six o'clock or later—when he saw his uncle coming. But the time had passed quickly. Even topping the excitement of gold to be dug was the new sensation of warmth toward his father. He couldn't put a finger on it—the mask still hid his father's face. But there had been the least small signs of the man beneath—a tired fellow who had accepted a favor from him. It almost revived that old, faded hope—

He was going back over their short talk for the tenth time when he saw Hep coming. The pudgy man was hurrying, dark-rimmed glasses askew, little mustache twitching. As he came up the last short climb, puffing and wheezing, he called breathlessly.

"Billy about?"

"No, sir. He's gone home an hour ago. Asked me to wait and give you this." Andy handed him the piece of tar paper, but Hep hardly glanced at it. Still breathing hard, he sank down on the big beam that braced the foot of the gallows frame.

"What else did he say? Anything?"

"Just that you'd have to go down the ladder because you're late."

"Ah, yes, I can imagine." Hep fanned himself rapidly with his hat. He looked a little sick—he was a sort of greenish color. "It's human nature, nephew, to find fault in others when you're trying to hide something yourself. My own brother—leaving you here to spy on my arrival. Oh, I don't know—I don't know—"

It disconcerted Andy to think he appeared to be spying. "No such thing, sir. Father said the chart was important."

"Oh, don't be shocked, lad. Billy's real reasons are hard to reckon. Even I can't fathom 'em, and I know him better than anyone. Shouldn't say it, I guess, but one gets tired of trying to help and always being blamed for things. Here I've spent the afternoon endeavoring to learn what new trouble's afoot. If I just had a hint of what he's got up his sleeve—" He broke off, staring at Andy. "Has he told you? Has he let fall any word of what he's up to? You're a quick lad—you've got a good head. Think!"

Andy thought—instantly. Of the bank holdup. He'd almost managed to put it out of his mind. Now he asked uneasily, "What makes you so sure there's trouble?"

His uncle evidently sensed something from his face. "Ah, so you do know!"

"No, sir. I don't know anything."

"Is it about this mine? The whole thing makes me suspicious—getting us into a backbreaking lot of labor on a worthless hole in the ground. Mining low-grade ore by hand is like trying to eat soup with a toothpick. You'll starve. I tell you, nephew, I've got to know what scheme is brewing, or I can't help him. You can trust me. What is it? What does Billy know that he's not telling?"

Andy could only shake his head.

Hep sighed. "You won't say—you don't want to inform against him. Ah, well, lad, I don't blame you. Many's the time I've done the same thing. It's just that I fear much is at stake here." He hunched over his elbows grimly. "Go on home, then. Tell Billy I finally showed up at six-thirty. Tell him I was detained by a small incident in town—ran into an acquaintance of ours. Or, rather, took good care *not* to run into him. I saw him before he saw me." With a wan smile he added, "I'm referring to that pillar of the law, Sheriff Duke Dade."

Eleven

Andy figured that supper would be over by the time he reached the house, but it didn't matter. Ever since Uncle Hep's news he hadn't felt very hungry. And if he had, his appetite would have been ruined by the smell of something burned which greeted him as he opened the front door. From the kitchen came the sound of angry voices.

Josey was yelling in high-pitched indignation, "Papa Miserable, you do not understand! The French *cuisine* is the most superb in all the world!"

"I noticed you didn't eat none of that junk, young lady." Old Misery looked ready to give off smoke himself, as Andy came into the room. On the table was a dish of something that still faintly smouldered.

"What is it?" he asked, wrinkling his nose.

"It is my crêpes suzette," Josey told him woefully.

"It's burnt eggs, that's what it is," Misery snapped.

"It smells worse than that," Andy said.

"That's because she sneaked some of my tanglefoot and put on it," the old man fumed.

"Your whisky?"

"But certainly!" Josey tossed her head. "I do not have any brandy. Always in France one cooks with brandy."

"She poured it all over the dern eggs, set the whole works afire, and calls that supper. Ought to turn her over m' knee." Misery eyed the girl wishfully.

Josey drew back, her eyes dark with defiance. "Do not try this, *mon papa!*"

The old man shook a finger at her. "You clean up this mess, and tomorrow I expect good plain food fit for the table or you're out of a job."

Josey went switching off to the sink, and Misery beckoned Andy out of the kitchen. When they were alone he sighed.

"Never could do nothin' with women. Here, skipper, go downtown and buy yourself some proper victuals. Some beans, maybe—" he pressed a silver dollar into Andy's hand.

"I've got to speak to my father first."

"He's gone on to town. Remi, too. They couldn't handle her neither, I reckon. When them eggs went up in smoke, everybody scattered. Dern little fool, she could've blowed the roof off the house. That tanglefoot is stronger'n battery acid."

As Andy headed for town the emptiness in him was

too vast for any food to fill. It seemed as though just when everything was starting to go right, it had to go all wrong again. Even the household was in a mess, and he had to admit ruefully that it was his own fault for bringing the lot of them together. He tried to think what to do with Josey. There was really no way to control a small cat, except, of course, to get a bigger cat.

With a twinge of anguish he wished again for the nice, safe, comfortable world of animals, where everything was logical. People were such—people. Restlessly he roamed up one side street and down another, peering into restaurants, wondering where his father might have gone and what would happen if he were to come face to face with Duke Dade. He knew the sheriff of one county couldn't arrest anybody in another sheriff's county, but it seemed likely they were all friends and would do each other any little favor.

It was late by the time he had covered the town without any luck. Andy knew he should go back home. Victor was taking on a new pitch—the raucous sound of night laughter and racy music and raw words. Men—the same men who had tramped off shift with stubbled faces and dirty clothes a few hours ago—now strutted the street in bowler hats and shiny black gabardine pants; candy-striped shirts and string ties and a cheroot hanging aslant from a grinning mouth. But the scarred, callused hands were ready to knock anybody's block off. Andy wondered, longingly, if he would ever be that tough.

He noticed that people looked at him curiously. It

was certain there were few boys his age on the streets at this hour. And yet, he thought, there was one thing more he might do. Likely his father had gone home, all unaware of any danger. But it might be helpful if Andy could at least locate where Duke was staying. He was sure his father would want to know that.

Keeping clear of the crowds as much as possible, he headed for the biggest hotel in town. A party was going on there, handsome people all over the lobby—too many for him to go in and ask questions. He decided to mosey over to another, smaller hotel that he remembered seeing on a side street. And there Andy found him.

From half a block away he recognized the man seated on the veranda. The big white Stetson, the massive, handsome figure—there was no mistaking Duke Dade. He was seated with some other men; the whole scene was plain as day under the gas lamps that lit the porch. As Andy moved quietly closer he could even see the big silver belt buckle that had flashed in the torchlight those awful few minutes at the stage station in Black Hawk. The rumble of the deep voice came to him indistinctly. He wished he could hear what they were saying. . . .

There were some bushes at the edge of the veranda. Cautiously Andy crept toward them through the deep shadows, doubled over, until he was right under the porch railing, not ten feet from the sheriff himself. The talk was disappointing—just about this and that, the way men will. A young fellow in a black shirt was asking Duke what he thought of Cripple Creek.

"The district or the town? I've never seen a finer

little community—nice folks over there. But this district—" Duke shook his head.

"What's the matter with it? Richest camp in the West."

"Oh, you've got big holdings here—no doubt about that. Big problems to go along with 'em." Duke bit the end off a cigar and spat it so close to where Andy was hidden, he nearly moved and gave himself away. He knew he should get out of there, but a sort of fascination held him. There was something terrible and awesome about this man who was his father's sworn enemy.

"Crime, for instance," Duke went on. "It's hard to bring under control in a boom as big as this town's had. Where we've been able to run out the grifters, you still have 'em. I'd say, from talking to your own sheriff this afternoon, that you're overrun with all sort of bunco artists, holdup men, high-graders, sneak thieves of every variety, one of whom I suspect"—he got to his feet, stretching lazily—"is hiding right here!" Quick as a gunshot he had vaulted the railing and laid hold of Andy's collar. "Come on out in the light, fellow. Let's have a look at you."

No use to try to twist away from that grip. Andy cast about hastily for some good excuse to explain his presence.

"Now then—" Duke turned him to face the porch lights. For the first time Andy could see the cold blue glint of the sheriff's eyes. "Just a boy. What the devil were you up to, hiding there?"

"I just wanted to see what you looked like," Andy

answered rapidly. "Heard folks say you were a big lawman from Black Hawk. Sorry I bothered you—I'll go home now, if you don't mind."

Duke smiled slightly; then the handsome face narrowed. "Wait a minute. There's something familiar about that hat—let's see what's under it." Swiftly he skimmed the old straw from Andy's head and recognition dawned in his face. "Well, well, well. So that's it. Now it becomes clearer. This lad's a dead ringer for his pappy—a gent with whom I've had some dealings that weren't pleasant at all."

The young bucks on the porch were interested.

"Never mind, it's a long story," Duke told them. "Started years ago in Central City, in my greenhorn days, when a couple of sharpers sold me a salted mine. It's a shame, though, that they've turned the boy into a night skulker. Go on"—abruptly he released Andy—"get home and tell your father whatever you think you've picked up. Tell him I said it's a worse crime than thieving—to ruin a kid."

Jamming his hat on his head furiously, Andy marched off down the street, aware of the laughter behind him. His fists were clenched—he could've killed somebody! And the worst of it was, he had only himself to thank. Hadn't figured on those keen eyes of Duke's. Hadn't figured how fast he could move, either. Hadn't figured *anything* right.

He dreaded to think how this whole business would

look to his father. That mockery would come back to haunt him. Maybe he wouldn't let him go down in the mine. Maybe they wouldn't even stay in town any more, with Duke on the trail. They'd have to go on the run again—what about this "salted" mine? Where would it all end, anyhow? Burning inside, Andy rushed along the street not caring who he jostled.

He had almost reached the corner where he would turn toward home when something made him glance back. A dark shirt, there in the crowd, caught his eye— mainly because it ducked aside and got behind some people when he looked back. Curiously Andy moved on, past his corner and down to the next where he paused, pretending to look in a hockshop window. The black shirt was back there all right—leaning casually against a lamp post. For a minute he didn't figure it. Even if that was the fellow who had been on the porch with Duke, why should he be following—? And then it hit him like a load of rock. Duke must have sent someone after him to find out where he lived. It would be very handy—for him to lead the way to his father.

If he'd been mad before, Andy was twice as mad now. Strolling along to the next side street, he stepped around the corner and waited. A minute later Black Shirt came charging around in a hurry so as not lose him. Andy stuck out a foot. The fellow stumbled and whirled.

"You're wasting your time," Andy said between clenched teeth. "Now get on out of here and leave me alone." It was a bluff—the other boy was at least three or four years older and twenty pounds heavier, but at that point Andy didn't care.

"You talk big for a little squirt," Black Shirt said thinly. He didn't like being tripped.

"You're pretty much of a squirt, yourself. Go on back, tell Duke he's ruining a little kid, turning you into a sneaky-Dick."

And Black Shirt hit him. With his open hand he slapped hard. Jarred sideways, Andy struck out with his fist—it was like hitting a block of wood. Black Shirt grunted a curse and jabbed—it caught Andy across the cheek and spun him around. He went down onto hands and knees, the world wheeling before his eyes. Two legs came to stand in front of his blurred vision.

"Get up, squirt."

Beneath the fancy pegged trousers the long shins were clad in black hose. Andy grabbed them and yanked. Black Shirt came down, with a foul oath. Scrambling up, Andy ran—along the side street, into an alley, stumbling along blindly over the rutted roadway. On across another street and into the pitch-dark of the next alley. Midway down it he clattered over a trash can and fell. As he got up, he looked back. Behind him a long-legged figure was silhouetted against the light. It lunged after him.

And Andy knew he wasn't going to make it.

Twelve

As Black Shirt came for him, Andy flattened against the wall. And then, abruptly, between the two of them a shaft of light sliced across the darkness of the alley. A back door had opened, letting forth a rush of noise—woman chatter and tinny piano music. Two men came out, making a good deal of racket themselves, singing some song. Without stopping to weigh the consequences, Andy ducked past them and went in. As soon as the door closed he shot the bolt on the inside, then stood with his back against it, breathing hard.

He found himself in a short passageway that led to a big hall up front. Bright lights there, and a dazzling array of people. Women, dressed in the finest possible clothes, their hair piled on top of their heads, handsome jewels on their hands and dangling from their ears; and men, dancing these gorgeous ladies around to the fastest tune Andy had ever heard. The piano player was seated at his instrument on a raised platform so that everybody could see him. A weird figure—spidery thin, dressed in narrow black pants and a striped satin shirt, his sleeves held up by gaudy red garters—but his hands moved like magic, racing over the keys, spreading a torrent of music.

Up near the front was a bar where more men waited their turn with the ladies. When Andy saw that, he was practically certain—this was one of those places that the men back in Kansas had referred to as a "Den of Iniquity." He'd always wanted to see the inside of one. Now as he moved along the hallway for a better look a door right ahead of him opened and one of the handsome young women walked out. When she saw Andy she gasped.

He was just as amazed at the sight of her. It was like looking into a doll's face, white with powder, painted over with rouge. There were blue lines penciled on her eyelids and her hair was a shade of red he'd never seen on a human being. Up close, it was plain to see that the sparkling stones in her necklace were just colored glass. But what jolted him most was her voice.

"Holy mackerel! A kid!" She said it in a flat twang, so familiar it was like being home in Kansas. "Where the devil did you come from?"

"The alley." Andy glanced down at himself and saw that his shirt was bloody and dirty—that's what she was staring at. "I'm sorry to bust in this way, but a fellow was chasing me."

"Looks like he already caught you."

"Yes, ma'am—once. He's probably gone now, but do you reckon I could go out the front way?"

"Not looking like that, you can't. If the manager saw you he'd have a conniption. Come on in here and clean up." She took his arm and led him into the room she had just left. It seemed to be a dressing room, all sorts of flouncy feminine clothes were hanging around on hooks. There were several couches and chairs—he guessed the ladies must come back here to rest between dances.

"Hurry now"—she was pouring water into a basin—"even if you are only a young'un, men aren't allowed in here."

Andy sloshed his face, but his nose was beginning to bleed again. It kept getting on his shirt. "Thank you, but I guess I'd better just go on out the rear," he said, though he had an awful hunch Black Shirt was still there.

"And get yourself killed?" She shook her head angrily. "Don't be a dunce. Makes me sore—what are your parents thinking of, to let a kid run around this late at night in a rough town like this? I swear I'd like to give 'em a piece of my mind!"

"I didn't tell my father I was coming," Andy protested. "Anyhow, I was going home, except that this fellow was following me and I didn't want him to see where I live."

"You ought to have your tail walloped." She was unbuttoning his shirt as if she were his mother or something. "Come on, we've got to wash the blood off it before you can go out there. Put a cold washcloth on the back of your neck. Tip your head back—here, like this!" She sat him down in a chair with a wet rag clamped to his neck, then went back to the basin. "Probably get me fired," she muttered to herself. "Not that I'd give a hoot. This is a rotten way to earn a living—men shoving a girl around the floor, stepping all over her feet. You'll be just like 'em in a few years, rough and rude. It's too bad, a nice kid going to the dogs, running loose in the alleys at midnight. Makes me mad."

"Listen, I *had* to," he retorted. "My father's in danger. I had to warn him."

"That's what I mean—danger." She wrung the shirt out fiercely. "It's a crime, if you got kids, to live in a place where there's danger all around. Your mother ought to lay down the law, that's what."

"I haven't got a mother," Andy said quietly.

She didn't speak, just looked around at him, and for an instant a softness showed in her eyes. Then from far away they heard the music come to an end. The woman frowned a little and went across to lock the door. Coming back to his side, she said, "How's the nose?"

Andy sat up straight and felt of it gingerly. "Stopped bleeding, I think."

"Here's your shirt. It's wet, but it's clean—you can get by with it. You're going to have a mouse under that eye." She was scolding, but the touch of her hand on his cheek was almost longing. "Gosh you're bony. I'll bet they never give you a square meal. You haven't got half the beef on you that my kid brother had, last time I saw him." She smiled a little. "I've got a kid brother—somewhere. Bet you don't believe that. Dance-hall girls aren't supposed to have families."

People were coming now, voices right outside the door. Somebody tried the knob.

"Say, who's in there? Open up!" Girls' voices were clamoring.

"Go away," she said. "I've got a headache." In an undertone she added, "And that's no lie."

"It's Adeline!"

"Adeline's locked herself in the dressing room." All sort of fuss was being raised now. A heavier fist hit the door.

"Adeline, you open up and do it quick!" A man's voice.

"That's the manager," Adeline told Andy between shut teeth. "I hate his spats!"

"Who's in there with you? Open up this minute."

She made a face at the door. To Andy she said, "Let me do the talking. You just ease on out front and keep going. Good luck."

"I'm grateful for your help." He had his shirt buttoned and tucked in—a look in the mirror reassured him. She had done a good job at restoring him. He slicked his hair back with his fingers. Adeline was unlatching the door. Next minute the room was full of people.

"Watcha doing? What's going on?" The manager

101

was a fussy little man in fussy clothes. He stared at Andy. "For the love of—!"

"This is my kid brother." Adeline confronted him, hands on hips. "You want to make a court case out of it?"

"Brother? You got a *brother?*"

Andy was doing as she'd instructed, moving slowly toward the door. They went on bickering—he heard Adeline say, "You know what you can do with this job in just about one minute?"

"Ah, go on, get out there on the floor. We got customers—*cash customers!*"

Hastily Andy made his way through the crowded outer room almost unnoticed. The men were ganged around the little gate that separated them from the girls between dances. They were all waving tickets and calling for partners. As Andy slipped on outside he gave a quick glance around, to make sure Black Shirt wasn't in sight, then hurried—almost ran—for home. Somehow the dance hall left a discomfort inside him worse than all the rest of the night's doings. He kept thinking of Adeline and the bushy-bearded mule skinners, the swaggering mine workers who would be waltzing her around and around and around. . . .

When he reached home the lights were all off except one, far back in the kitchen. Andy hesitated. He didn't want to talk to anybody, but whoever it was would be bound to hear him tiptoe up the creaking stairs. Better to go straight on in and get it over with. To his relief he found it was only Misery, sitting with his feet on the stove, reading the paper. Glancing over his shoulder, he took in the black eye and wrung-out shirt.

"Lose your hat?" he asked mildly.

"I reckon I did," Andy marveled. "Dern if I remember where."

"Must've been a pretty good scrap." The old man grinned.

"Not too good. He was bigger than me. I was mostly running."

"That makes sense." Misery got up and folded the paper. It dawned on Andy that the old man had been waiting up for him.

"I'm sorry I was so late," he said, and he meant it. "Did—didn't my father say anything about it?"

"He went to bed early. I told him not to worry about you, said you just stepped out for a bite of grub. Me, I almost got uneasy when you didn't come. This ain't a good town to go nighthawkin' in—but I reckon you found that out."

"Yes, sir." Andy was grateful that the old man wasn't going to ask him a lot of questions. He wasn't too proud of all the bumbling he had done. "Only good thing about it—maybe I located a cook for us."

Misery's shaggy brows cocked quizzically. "Where is she? I'll go down, hire her tomorrow early 'fore somebody else gits her. Cooks is scarcer in this town than feathers on a fish."

Andy said cautiously, "Her name is Adeline, and she's

one of the ladies in the Single-Jill Dance Hall."

The old man's fading eyes went wide with curiosity, though he still didn't pry. Just waited for Andy to go on.

"I think she can cook—at least she was worried about me not getting enough square meals."

"Sure sign." The old man nodded.

"And I *think* she's tired of her job."

"No doubt. Hard life on a woman." Misery was still waiting.

"But one thing I *know*"—Andy grinned wearily—"if anybody can handle Josey, she can."

Thirteen

There were a lot of things left unsaid that next morning. Misery didn't explain why he was heading for town instead of the mine. Andy's father had refrained from mentioning the black eye. And Andy decided not to say anything about Duke Dade or his whereabouts— might lead to a whole lot of questions. Besides, his father knew by now that the sheriff was in town. Andy had heard his uncle talking to him late last night, after Hep had got home from work. And this morning Brett was troubled. So sunk in his own thoughts he hardly responded to Remi's conversation as they went up the hill toward the mine.

"I only hope the man did not lie," the Frenchman was saying. "He promised to deliver the timber at sunrise."

Brett roused out of his musing. "I'd say he made good

his word. There's been a wagon up this road since we came down it last night."

Remi stared at the dirt with interest. "Billee, you are right! This I did not notice. You have quick eyes."

"Got to," Brett said distantly. "Dealing poker or busting rock, you're only a half-inch away from trouble."

Remi glanced over, his gray eyes wistful. "This is a thing I notice about America—so different from France where one lives warmly, graciously. In my country, one does not resort to physical violence." He glanced at Andy's shiner. Brett did too. Andy felt obligated to say something.

"I didn't resort to it," he told them sorely. "The other fellow started the fight."

His father seemed less disturbed than he'd expected. "Doesn't hurt a boy to get into a scrap or two. Once you know what it feels like to get hit, you're not afraid of it."

Remi looked uncomprehending.

"If we seem so strange to you," Brett went on, "how does it happen you wanted to come to this country, Remi?"

"Ah, gold!" The Frenchman laughed. "One understands that!"

They had reached the mine now. A stack of peeled logs had been left near the shaft. Brett looked them over.

"It's a two-man job, laying up timber, so we'll have to wait until Misery comes before we can do much work.

But maybe we can get some rock cleaned up in the meantime. Let's see what Hep's shot knocked down last night. Put on your headgear, boy."

Andy had been hanging onto the old helmet which Misery had unearthed from a back closet. Now he set it on his head—it felt strange and rigid, not too comfortable.

As they took their places on the skip, his father said, "Keep your elbows in or you'll be minus some skin."

And at that moment the cage plunged into the darkness. Silently it dropped, faster and faster, walls of rock racing past unseen, so close they brushed Andy's sleeve. Down . . . down . . . the black damp air getting colder, striking through the denim shirt, through his flesh to chill the core of his bone. And still the flimsy floor beneath their feet fell away into nothingness below. Hands knotted so tight they hurt, Andy held his breath. Cable must have broken—they were hurtling downward unchecked! And then the skip began to slow, gently settled to a stop as if there were no trick to it. He let out his pent-up breath and swabbed the perspiration from his forehead.

"Stay put until I get this candle lit," Brett said in the dark.

And now that his stomach was steadying down, Andy began to quicken inside. He had been waiting for this —he thought just about anything might happen. Somehow he felt that today was going to prove something about his "golden touch." It *had* to pretty soon, or he was going to start losing faith in it. Uncle Hep's shot would have left a big stripe of gold showing—at least he thought that's what a vein looked like, a layer of gleaming pure metal.

The small flame flickered to life, casting a weird glow up over his father's lean face. Brett handed him the candle and set about lighting another. It seemed a thin sort of illumination to combat such absolute darkness, but it was what they would work by. Each candle was stuck in an iron holder with a sharp spike sticking out —Andy held his gingerly as he stepped off the skip and looked around.

The bottom of the mine wasn't at all as he'd expected. No awesome cavern—just a small room carved out of rock with tools stacked around it, and leading away into the dark, a narrow tunnel hardly big enough to stand up in. The floor was the smoothest part. The sides were jagged rock and water dripped from the low, rough ceiling.

Stepping off the skip, his father jerked a cord—a bell rang once somewhere, and the cage rose out of sight, leaving them stranded here in the depths of the earth. Andy looked after it uneasily. He hoped nothing would go wrong with that bell. His father was picking up tools, tossing them into a wheelbarrow. As he started down the tunnel, wheeling it, he was talking along.

"Stick close to me and do just as you're told—no more nor less. This that you see around you is your chosen cell, boy—the place where you want to spend your days, sweating and shivering and swinging a pick till your muscles cramp and your joints swell. Blinking in darkness while upstairs the sun is out all over the place. But don't forget, there may be gold behind some of this rock. You may even get some, if it doesn't get you first."

"How could it 'get' me?" Andy swiped at a drip of cold water that had gone down his neck.

"Rockfall for one thing." Brett came to a halt. The tunnel was blocked by a pile of rubble that cascaded down out of a gaping hole in the side wall. "Just that much rock would bury you permanently."

"What made it come down?" Andy asked uneasily.

"In this case, explosive. This is the start of our drift —see those powder marks? That's where Hep set off his charge last night. By tonight we've got to have this rock cleaned up so that he can set some more powder. We've also got to brace this part of the tunnel with that timbering. Look up there—"

Across the rock ceiling some jagged cracks had spread out from the place where the powder had gone off.

"And this east wall has been tricky all along." Brett held up the lamp to look at it more closely. "That blast loosened it some more. We've got to keep our eye on it this morning. If you hear a groan or a little crackle deep in the rock, run for the shaft."

Andy nodded as cheerfully as he could.

"You look cold, but you'll soon work up some steam." Brett spiked his candle into a crack in the rock wall, then dumped the tools out of the wheelbarrow onto the floor—a shovel, several hand chisels, and a couple of large sledges. "While I knock down the loose, you can start tossing rock into that wheelbarrow."

Andy picked up the shovel—it wasn't the biggest one they had. He was a little irritated at his father, trying to baby him. But when he dug into the rock, he found it was a whale of a lot heavier than he had reckoned. And by the time he had the wheelbarrow filled, he was sweating. Just as glad the shovel wasn't too large, or he might have given out at the work.

"Don't try to handle that—it's a man's job." His father took the wheelbarrow and ran it back to the shaft to dump it into the big ore bucket that hung just below floor level there. When it was full, they would hook it to the bottom of the skip to be hoisted up top. But Andy could see it was going to take a while.

"This is just dump rock, isn't it?" he asked, the least bit discouraged.

"It is. And you'll shovel a thousand tons of it for every ton of pay-rock you load. Especially when you're opening a new drift."

Andy had been wondering about that. "But how do you know where to open it?"

"That's a good question. It takes years of looking at rock, as Misery has done, even to make a guess at where an ore shoot may occur. Especially in a place like this district where the gold doesn't lie in flat layers. It came into these rocks under pressure, forced up by the heat at the center of the earth, so that the veins run up and down. When all this was hot, a million years ago, the gold sprayed up and out into the cracks and pockets in the rock. A lot of it got mixed right in with the rock itself. That's why you can't see it in our low-grade ore —it's too diffuse. The point is to locate a vein or at least an offshoot; that's what we're going for here." As he talked, he swung the biggest sledge with both hands, hard, and loose rock fell with a crash.

"How soon do I learn to use that hammer?" Andy asked enviously.

"This"—his father swung again—"is a doublejack. The one-handed sledge is a singlejack. Both are too heavy for you to handle. And you're falling behind me farther every minute."

Hurriedly Andy dug into his own work. A pocket of pure gold, though—that would be something to see. And if it meant—working like this—on dump rock—he could certainly—do it—

When the bell sounded somewhere far above he thought it must be his ears ringing with fatigue. Leaning against the side of the tunnel, he wiped his face on his sleeve.

"I reckon that's the noon bell, maybe."

"Not more than ten o'clock." His father didn't check in his work. "That's probably Misery coming down."

It reminded Andy that there was a thing he'd wanted to ask his father while they were alone. And no telling how soon there would be another chance.

"That first day," he said, trying to sound casual,

"Misery said this mine might be 'salted.' What did he mean?"

Brett shot him a look as if suspecting a hidden reason for the question. At last he said, "Some people with Remi's lack of experience have bought worthless mines. They've been fooled by some swindler who has planted high-grade ore around a low-grade strike—or even where there has been no strike at all. A tenderfoot will grab up a chunk of the planted rock, take it to the assay office, and think he's buying a gold mine."

There was no time to ask more. The skip was down and Misery was hurrying along the tunnel, carrying his miner's candlestick in one hand, a piece of paper in the other. He looked worried.

"Didn't you get her?" Andy called.

"Oh, sure. No trouble there. She's already movin' her gear over to the house." As he came up the old man was out of breath and upset. "That ain't what kept me, it was your visitor, Bill."

Neither Andy nor his father spoke, but the name of a certain lawman hung in mid-air almost loud enough to be heard.

"Big fellow," Misery went on gloomily. "Wore a white Stetson and a black six-gun. Smelled all over like a sheriff. Asked a bunch of fool questions which, as I told him, was none of his danged business."

"What questions?" Brett asked between tight lips.

"Such as who my boarders was and where-at they could be found and when they would be home—oh, I never give him the time of day. But he's nobody's fool. He knows you hang your hat there. Wrote you a note— just pulled out a piece of paper, cool as grass, and stepped over to the porch table and wrote it." Misery was turning a folded scrap of paper around and around in his hands as if he were of a mind to throw it away.

Brett set the doublejack aside and came over to take the message. By the wavering candlelight he read it to himself. Then, with a shrug, handed the note to Misery —Andy read it over the old man's shoulder.

On hotel stationary, it was short. The writing was bold and flourishing and somehow so like the writer, it hardly needed the signature, which he had written with a single sweep of the pen: "Dade." The sentence itself was sparse enough:

"Billy Brett—either you come to see me tonight, or I'll come looking for you."

Fourteen

By afternoon of that day Andy was ready to admit that mining was a tough job. Pitching bundles under the sun was one thing—the fields had smelled good. Horses and dogs and men were in harmony with the summer and the growing wheat. Down here, under the earth, nothing seemed natural. The air was foul, even though the ventilator shaft was at this far end of the crosscut where he was working. But the light was the worst thing about being underground. After hours of the wavering glow, Andy felt as if his eyes were being squeezed. And this, in spite of the fact that they had given him a lamp with four candles in it to do some special work.

Alone here at the end of the tunnel, he hunkered down beside a pile of rock, picking through it piece by piece, tossing the granite aside, putting the darker fragments of sylvanite into the wheelbarrow. All afternoon this had been his chore while the men were struggling to set timber. They had made a structure to shore up the wall and ceiling of the tunnel, but Andy didn't think it looked too sturdy. The logs were only four or five inches thick. However, Misery said it was a good job. Andy could hear him talking now to Brett, their voices sounding hollow and distant.

He tried to take some satisfaction that at least he was working on gold—what little they had. The ore was just a streak of dark rock in the middle of the face of red granite—not a very wide streak, either. To break it up they used powder. But the shot had brought down both ore and granite. That was why he had to sort through the rubble. Squinting at one of the smaller pieces, Andy tossed it into the wheelbarrow.

A ton—it was hard to imagine how much a ton was. But when he had picked out a ton of ore it would be hauled to the mill where it would bring fifty dollars. Out of that would come ten for the freighter, another ten for powder and caps, some more for gasoline for the motor, timbering, tools to be sharpened. They would be lucky, his father said, if that ton of ore brought them twenty dollars net, to be divided among them. And even then it was only fair that Misery get a large share of it, to pay for the food they all ate. Furthermore, Remi owned the mine; he'd expect a good portion. Andy wondered if there would be any share for him at all, considering how small his part was.

He couldn't help remembering what Uncle Hep had

said—that this was a foolish way to waste time. And even his father admitted that Hep knew an awful lot about gold. It must be almost time for his uncle to come to work; it was on Andy's mind to ask him more about all this. Why, for instance, had they opened the drift in the middle of the tunnel instead of down here at the end where the sylvanite was?

But by the time Hep finally came, Andy could only think gratefully that it meant it was nearly five o'clock. His curiosity had petered out under a mountain of weariness. Dimly he heard the men exchange greetings; then saw his uncle coming along the tunnel. The fluttering light of the candle cast shadows up over his round, anxious face.

"Nephew, nephew!" He bent down and grasped Andy's shoulder with concern. "I'd not have believed this! To think that Billy would let a mere youngster work to the point of exhaustion! It's unhealthy enough for grown men to work in a fetid hole in the ground, but a growing boy—what the devil is he thinking of?"

"I asked for the job," Andy said doggedly. "Father didn't want me to come down."

Hep glanced over his shoulder, lowering his voice. "I don't pretend to know why he's chosen this particularly worthless venture to invest his time in. But to give in to your boyish enthusiasm—no matter how ardently you asked—ah, lad, it's wrong. The beginning of a wasted life. A bright lad like you should be preparing that keen mind of yours for a more intellectual future. It's just as well I went ahead with my plan—" He broke off. Brett was coming along the passageway.

"You can start drilling your holes back here, Hep," he said as he came up. "We'll have to keep knocking down some ore, even while we open the drift farther. Have to keep a little cash coming in."

"Confounded small." Hep grumbled as he took off his coat. From a pile of drills that was stacked nearby, he selected one and picked up the light one-handed sledge that rested against the wall. "I've no heart in this," he confessed to Andy in a hushed voice. "It's not practical. The work that will take me an hour to do by hand could be accomplished in a few minutes with a pneumatic drill if we had steam equipment. This was a poor venture, lad, but the poorest part of it will be the aftereffects on you, unless we can get you out of this trap." He set the sharp end of the drill against the rock and began to tap it with the sledge, turning the bit slowly as he struck it, around and around so that it began to bite into the rock.

"What plan were you—?" Andy began, but Hep stopped him by a quick gesture.

"Never mind that now. Wait until it bears fruit, nephew. But I tell you, as soon as I saw that sheriff and knew Billy was in Dutch again, I knew I had to try to help you. It's no fair to a helpless boy, to be up against the forces of evil. Don't worry, lad, bear up just a bit

117

longer. I should have news for you within a few days. Go along now, they're knocking off. You should have been up in that fresh air long ago."

So tired he could hardly drag one foot after the other, Andy followed the men to the skip. It seemed a hundred years since they had come plunging down. The return ride was steadier; the floor of the cage shoved upward smoothly, and they burst out into daylight—Andy had to shut his eyes against it for a minute.

The heat of the afternoon sun had warmed the water in the bucket. Never had it seemed so good to wash up. His clothes were crusty with rock dust, he noticed a little proudly. When he had finished drying off, he looked around to find his father watching him.

"So, you've had your first work day. Same thing happens tomorrow—and the next day. Seven days a week right now. Still want the job?"

"Yes, sir." And summoned up a brisk tone. "I—like working hard."

"That's good. Because there's wood to split when we get home. Water to be drawn for tomorrow. Or did you forget that the house chores still go on?"

"No, sir," Andy lied weakly. "I didn't forget." The fact was that it hadn't entered his head.

Brett put on his helmet and slung his coat over his shoulder. Misery had already started on ahead of them; Remi wasn't ready to leave yet. So the two of them fell in step silently. Andy was thinking of the firewood.

"As for me," his father went on, "I'm too tired to do

much work of an evening. And I'd not let you do more than I would. That's why—whether you like it or not—you're going to hit the sack tonight. Tomorrow will be time enough for chores, because you'll be staying home. You can work in the mine every other day and no more. That's final. No arguments."

In a flood of relief Andy agreed humbly, "No arguments." And when he glanced at his father he thought he caught the glint of a smile about that sober face. It dawned on him that maybe his father was the least bit satisfied with him. It brought a tide of warm emotion that he could hardly comprehend.

They caught up with Misery, and the two men fell to talking about the drift. But it was evident that the old man was disturbed by something else. After some hem and haw, he finally said it outright.

"Bill, what ye aim to do about that sheriff feller?"

Brett didn't answer at once. At last he asked, "What would you do?"

Misery snorted. "Me? I never yet went searchin' out trouble."

"And I've never made a practice of hobnobbing with lawmen." Brett yawned wearily. "I think tonight I'll go to bed early."

They had reached the house now. Andy was slogging along, half asleep, and didn't rouse much until they came up the front steps. Then all three of them stopped short. Because from the open door came a fragrance. A mouth-watering, nose-twitching, heart-stopping mixture

of aromas . . . the smell of pot roast . . . homemade bread
. . . and fresh apple pie.

Brett stared at Misery dumfounded. But the old man
was grinning at Andy in congratulation.

"I swear-to-Harry," he said, "I think the boy found
us a cook!"

Fifteen

"In France," Josey said delicately, "one roasts the chicken. All in one piece, you know."

"Here"—Adeline brought the cleaver down expertly and the breast of the fowl lay split upon the cutting board—"here, we chop 'em up and fry 'em. At least that's what I'm going to do today." Whack—and the drumstick left the upper joint. She was a rapid cook, going at it like a man shoes horses. Andy, filling the wood box near the stove, glanced over at her in a certain admiration. There was nothing he knew how to do that well, with such sureness.

She made a somewhat different picture than she had the other night. The plain gingham dress was almost severe, buttoned up high at the neck. With all the paint scrubbed off her face she was pale as grass that's grown in the dark of a cellar. Her lips were bloodless and her brows seemed thin without the pencil marks. No jewelry at all—not a trace of glitter. Even the brilliant red hair was snubbed back under a dustcap. Only a few curly tendrils had sprung loose around her face. She brushed at them crossly as she worked.

Beside her, Josey looked small and fragile. She belted her dresses too tight, in Andy's opinion, and the gowns themselves, though much mended, were frothy with lace and ribbons. It made her seem more delicate than she was.

"Please," she was saying airily, "at least allow me to suggest the herbs."

Adeline shrugged. "You want some sage in the gravy, you can go out back and pick some."

"Sage!" Josey flung her hands and tossed her shock of light hair. "Raw—green—ugly—wild—sagebrush—sage!"

"Don't snap your mainspring," Adeline advised her calmly. "I'd just as soon settle for salt and pepper, myself."

"*Eh bien*," Josey sighed, "if one must be dull. But you may give me the liver. I will make us a small *paté de fois gras*. At least that will have flavor." She made a snatch at the chicken parts and Adeline slapped her hand away.

"That liver goes in the gravy, Miss. You keep out of my cooking or I'll patty your fwa-gras with a razor strap."

Josey looked at her with wide-eyed fury. Adeline stared her right back, floury hands dug into her hips,

brown eyes shooting sparks. Step by step Josey retreated—spinning around, she ran from the room and
Adeline turned back to her work, muttering.

". . . booby hatch!"

For all that he was glad enough the cookery had
changed hands, Andy couldn't help feeling a prick of
sympathy for Josey. He knew what it was to try a thing
and fail. It made him feel guilty to think that he had
got her into all this. And so, cautiously, he followed into
the upper reaches of the old house. He could hear her
tiptoeing up the stairs to the attic. Little ruffled cats
always steal away to some hidden spot, to crouch and
growl. The least he could do was try to smooth her fur
back in place.

The door at the top of the steps was closed, but as he
came up silently he heard a faraway tinkling sound from
within. Opening it, he saw her hunched down beside a
square wooden box. The lid was up and a metal cylinder
was turning, giving off small mechanical music. It was
a wistful little melody. Andy strolled over and sat down
on the floor nearby. Josey looked at him through her
tears, as if defying him to make fun of her.

"That's pretty," he said. "I've never heard that tune
before."

"It is 'The Plumes of Normandie,' " she told him in a
muted voice. "Normandie—it is in France."

He nodded and then sat still until the box ran down
and the attic was quiet.

"Shall I wind it up again?"

She shook her head. "I can only listen a little, or I

want to die. Almost I wish sometimes I did not find the music box at all."

"You must be homesick," he said. And then because it looked as though she might cry some more, he tried to get her talking. "How did you happen to come here so far from home?"

"How? I stowed myself away, as they say. On the boat. Remi was coming to this great place, America, and I wanted to see it." Head still buried against her knees she spoke into the folds of her skirt, the words coming muffled, as she told of the trip and the long ride across a strange land. "They said we would find gold. I thought I would have a gold ring, bracelets—and I will!" She raised her head fiercely. "I will make this cruel country give me something!"

"It's not so cruel," Andy argued. "Anybody can run into hard times anywhere."

"It is. It is *sauvage!* That woman, she struck me! And it is your fault—I heard Papa Miserable say you found her. You didn't like my cooking." She was getting mad, and that was better than tears, Andy thought.

"She needed a job—"

"She could find one herself. She is the bold kind," Josey cried scornfully. "No, it was my cooking. I hate you for that!"

"Aw, Josey, there's no disgrace in having to learn a thing. I've got to learn gold mining and—"

"Do not compare yourself with me," she warned him violently. "I am from a fine old family with great tradition. You are nothing but the son of a laborer. Your father is not even honest!"

That jolted Andy. He knew his father had told Remi about the Black Hawk trouble, but it had been done quietly. He was certain Josey couldn't know—or was it a guess?

"You care to explain what you meant by that?" he asked quietly.

"Only last evening," she said tartly, "he tells us all he is going to bed. You heard him say this? Then why, *mon petit* Andrew, why is it that when I stand at my window late, to look at the night sky, I see the figure of your parent descending from his room by means of the porch lattice? An unusual way to depart, except for thieves and rogues. Ha! You are so good at explaining everything to me, explain this!"

Andy met her look squarely. "I don't have to. My father's business is his, not yours. If you really have all that old tradition, you'll keep still about other people until you've got something worth saying." Getting to his feet, he left her sitting there, looking a little abashed.

As he went slowly downstairs Andy felt sore—at himself, for ever having been sorry for her. At his father, for making him stay home today and cope with a bunch of females. At Josey, for telling a darn-fool lie. But in his heart Andy felt sorest because he knew that it . . . probably . . . was no lie.

All the way to the store that afternoon he was quiet. Try as he might, he couldn't make much comment to Adeline's brisk remarks.

"Had to hide the fool chicken where she couldn't find it. The brown betty, too. She was bound I should spike it with some of the old man's liquor. I don't hold with that. Just hope she can't think of some way to doctor the bread I left rising."

"If she does," Andy remarked broodingly, "you've got my approval to whale the tar out of her." He had asked Uncle Hep what *petit* meant. The nerve of that *child*, calling him "little"!

"Reckon if I was to touch her," Adeline mused wishfully, "that brother of hers would skin me. He's a cool one. Looks at me as if I were mildew."

"They've got family tradition. Rest of us don't," Andy informed her.

"Oh, is that so? Well, my great-uncle Bisbee was a captain in the Army of the Potomac, and my own father rode shotgun on the Deadwood Stage, so I reckon I don't have to bow to anybody."

Andy nodded enviously. "I wish my—" He broke off, but she looked to him to go on. "I mean, I wish that somebody would explain things like that to Remi. He doesn't understand us—everybody. The whole country."

"No point in explaining. If a man wants to understand a thing he can. If he doesn't want to, he won't." She laughed a little bitterly. "Oh, I learned a-plenty about men these last couple of years."

It occurred to Andy that this must certainly be true. Choosing his words carefully, he said, "Did you ever wonder whether somebody was honest or not?"

"I'd be a dead duck if I hadn't."

"How could you tell?"

She glanced down thoughtfully. "You listen. While they talk you listen for false notes. Sooner or later you can piece it together. That is, if you've got a brain and use it."

"But suppose they don't talk much."

"You listen twice to everything," she said sardonically, "and think ten times as hard. Those are the kind to watch."

They had reached the market now. Adeline led the way inside with just the least switch of skirts, as if she were ready for trouble. Andy saw some of the other women give her a look, as if they knew she was an ex-dance-hall girl, but the storekeeper was polite enough.

Andy stood to one side and waited. What she had just said made him feel foolish, as though somehow he hadn't been very smart. Listen? Well, he'd been listening yesterday when his father had said he wasn't going to go to see Duke Dade. And yet, if he'd changed his mind and didn't want to answer a lot of questions, there wasn't any law against going down the lattice. Goodness knows the stairs creaked so loudly, you couldn't get past Misery and the others by going that way.

Adeline was beckoning him now. He went to take the basket from her, slung the sack of potatoes over his shoulder. As they walked along the street toward home he burst out.

"But honest men—do they ever lie?"

"Everybody lies sometime," she said. "What's bothering you, kid? Who are you wondering about—somebody in that household at home?"

He shook his head—and it struck him that even such a small gesture could be a lie.

"Sometimes you wonder," she was going on, "how people all get caught together in one place—me and you and the rest. It's fate, I guess. All here for one reason, gold. And all of us caught in the crusher."

The way she said it made Andy shudder, knowing as he did just how fate had operated in this instance. "What crusher?"

She laid a hand on his arm and jerked her head, as if she expected him to hear something. He listened—nothing special about the late-afternoon quiet. A few birds; some talk down the street.

"Don't you feel it?" she asked softly.

And then he knew what she meant—that rumbling vibration underfoot that went on and on, like huge wheels turning. The same throbbing hidden thunder that he had wondered about before.

"What is it, anyhow?"

"Those are the crushers, the big grinders that go on turning, day and night, chewing the rock up into mud. Trap the gold out of it and let the rest run into the ditch —worthless tailings. That's us when this place gets through with us, kid. Broken-down junk that's gone through the mill."

Sixteen

Sunday morning turned off quiet and hot. So still that Andy could hear the rumble of the crushers, even here in the shade of the old front porch, blocks away. All week since his talk with Adeline the sound had seemed to haunt him. When he walked along a street he could hear it through the other noise of traffic. It reached him now like the hushed breathing of something lying hidden close by.

Sitting on the porch steps, slumped over his knees, Andy tried to stop thinking about it. But it was no comfort to listen, instead, to the sounds that came from within the house. Back in the kitchen Adeline and Josey were squabbling. Upstairs somewhere Misery and Remi were arguing; their voices sounded angry in the distance. All of them victims of the same illusion—the pursuit of the "golden touch."

That must have been what his father was trying to warn him of, with those mocking comments about gold fever. Of all people, Bill Brett had probably felt the rough edge of the crushing wheels. Those remarks of his about danger, below ground and above. And what it feels like, to be hit. How many times had life dealt him some staggering, unexpected blow? Such as the early death of a wife—? For the thousandth time Andy wondered what his father must have been like in those days when a fine, gentle woman had chosen to marry him. The thought made an ache inside him, like a wish that can't come true. Because whatever he might have been once, the fact was that Will Brett now was a taciturn, loveless man.

All week he had been sunk in some depth of thought; hardly spoke, but drove himself at work with a sort of desperation. Right now he was up at the mine. Although the others had tried to get him to take a day off, he had brushed them aside with a curt word and gone. It was as if he were suddenly in some grim tension. And only Andy had the least inkling as to why. . . .

He glanced up at the leaves dangling motionless from the vine that grew along the porch lattice. At the corner a large patch was torn loose, small broken tendrils trailing down. A slat in the trellis was splintered off short— a fresh wound in the old gray weathered wood. Of course, there's no law against climbing down a porch lattice, he claimed again fiercely to the silence. Probably just coincidence that it was the very same night that Duke Dade had disappeared.

Andy had asked around—nobody had seen the sheriff since that evening. Of course, he might have decided to go back to Black Hawk or—anywhere. But somehow Andy couldn't make himself believe it. Nor could he help connecting this with the black mood that had been on his father ever since. He wished there were someone he could talk to. He'd never felt more alone in the world. But this was a thing no one could help him on. No one would care, unless—?

He had just caught sight of Hep. The little man was coming up the street. When he saw Andy he waved something—a sheet of paper. As he drew nearer it was plain to see that he was pleased. Behind the black-rimmed glasses his bright eyes were keen with delight; even his mustache seemed to curl with satisfaction.

"News!" he called as he came up the front walk. Sinking down on the steps beside Andy, he clapped an arm about the boy's shoulders. "The news I've been hoping for. It's come! You're saved, my lad. The whole world is yours—no more grubbing and sweating in the dirt. No more fear of the law. No more agonizing suspicions about your father's strange doings—"

"I'm not suspicious," Andy protested, in sheer defense against his secret misgivings.

"Bravo, my boy! Loyal to the end. Full of pride. Oh, the family is going to take to you, nephew. I know it."

"Whose family?"

"Yours, of course." He chuckled, fanning himself with the piece of paper. "You have one, even though your father forsook them long ago and never has even written them of your existence. I've tried to mind my own business, but when I see an innocent boy being denied his rightful heritage—well, nephew, I felt it my duty to write your grandparents. And here is their answer. They want you, lad. They welcome you. They'll care for you, send you to school—our family's well off, y'know. On to college—you'll have a chance to use that eager young mind. With your quick wit, I don't doubt you can become anything you choose!"

Andy could hardly take it in. Dazed, he turned the envelope over in his hands—it was postmarked "Virginia." Written in beautiful style, the letter wasn't long but it sounded warm enough. His grandparents were shocked to learn that Will had a son, but were anxious to take him in. "The poor child must be removed from the crude life that his father has chosen to lead," they wrote. That goaded him, somehow.

"My father's not crude!"

"No, no, of course not," Hep agreed. "But you must admit, my boy, that these surroundings are hardly refined. Nor is it a dignified occupation, grubbing in the earth."

Andy finished the letter and folded it. He didn't know what to say. Whole whirling visions were going through his head—of some handsome school with plenty of books in it and nice people around who always spoke quietly. Of learning to do worthwhile things, such as write letters as fine as this one.

"If it's the thought of gold making you hesitate," Hep

went on, "let me tell you, nephew, I've seen men who have chased that will-o'-the-wisp a whole lifetime and ended with empty pockets and an emptier soul. The true metal lies in a man's heart and mind. When he turns aside in search of gold dust he kills the precious treasure within him. Look around you, lad, at these ruined people—old Misery, poor Adeline, look at me and your father—"

"My father's not ruined!" Andy found himself arguing, even against good reason. "He's just—somehow, he's in trouble. If that sheriff hadn't come sneaking around, pestering him, everything would have been all right!"

"Do you think so? Poor lad, I can certainly understand your confusion." Hep nodded sadly. "I've been going through it for years. Ever since I, myself, was an impressionable boy, idolizing an older brother, casting my fate with his. Always hoping for the best. Well, no matter, I'm just a fumbling, lazy old cuss now. But you're young—your life lies ahead. You'll be given all the opportunities I squandered. You'll learn the richness of our culture, music, the arts, fine literature. Ah, think what your mother would whisper to you if she were here. She'd not want you to miss this chance."

Up to then Andy had almost been swayed by the persuasive words. But he knew for certain what his mother would say. "She'd not want me to leave my father."

Hep looked sober. "I think she would, lad, if she knew how careless he's been of your welfare."

"No, sir. He's always protecting me—he didn't want me to go to work. He won't even let me swing the pick yet. He's done the best he could—he even risked his life to come to town and fin'd me at the stage station that first night. Now he's probably risking it some more, to get money for us to live on." It came spilling forth from some place where the words must have been dammed up for a long time. It eased some terrible tightness in him, just to shout it out. "I don't want to leave my father!"

Hep rubbed his chin thoughtfully. "I didn't realize that you were old enough to appreciate what a sacrifice it has meant for Billy to accept the responsibility of caring for a son. But in your admirable effort to be dutiful, aren't you overlooking one thing? Oh, he would never mention it—neither would I, except to prove to you that you can go to your grandparents with a free conscience. I'm referring now to your father's own safety. As you point out, he has risked his neck and is still on dangerous ground, yet he can't just vanish into the night, hop a freight, and seek a new life. He must stay and take his chances of jail—or worse. Who knows? In a way, you see, you'd be doing him a favor, to go."

The minute of elation Andy had felt was flickering down to ashes. It was true enough. He was well aware that his coming had made his father's whole life more difficult. Before he could answer, though, a cowbell began to clang. Adeline, calling them to dinner.

As they sat down at the table, the others were still bickering. Misery was shaking a finger at Remi.

134

"When you learn to handle a singlejack, buster, you can ask me for explanations."

The Frenchman looked hot and explosive. "Sir, it is my mine. I have the right to ask where we are going with this drift. I have surveyed the direction—you are not even working at a right angle to the crosscut. Did you realize this?"

"Do I know? You askin' me if I know where-at I'm *at!*" Misery yelled.

"Hey, now, food's on." Adeline set a steaming platter of steaks before them and took a seat at the table. "Everybody start passing things."

"I simply say," Remi went on with an air of injury, "that I would like to understand your reasonings. The drift is costing money—"

"Money that you'd not have if Bill and Hep and me wasn't down there bustin' rock." Misery dug into the mashed potatoes angrily.

"But why will you not tell me?" Remi insisted. "Unless there is some reason you do not wish me to know—?"

"By cootie, are you accusin' me of double-dealin'?" Misery slapped his fork down. "It's just I got no time to try to teach minin' to a little book-totin' school kid—"

"Sir, I am a university graduate!"

"Oh, stop it, fellows," Adeline tried again. "Quit your jawin' and eat your dinner."

"If this food had more elegance," Josey remarked sweetly, "the gentlemen would eat with good appetite. You would not have to coax."

"I've had about enough of that kind of talk." Adeline shook a spoon at her across the table. "If you don't like the victuals, sissy-girl, you can go right on out in the kitchen and fix your own."

Remi reddened, quivering with insult. "This is intolerable. That a servant should speak so—!"

"*Servant?*" Misery roared. "Just because a body's useful, Mister Remi, don't make 'em a servant, and you'd better be findin' that out. In fact, I cut Addie in on my share of the mine, right here and now. She's a partner and a member of this family, same as all of us."

"Family? Family?" Josey let out a peal of furious laughter. "I think I do not belong to such a family. It is a madhouse!" Leaping up, she ran from the room. Remi followed.

Adeline, pale as a sheet, picked up her plate and went into the kitchen. Misery's old face crumpled, the spark going out of it. Dully he stared at the food on the table, then got up and shuffled off toward the front of the house, fumbling in his pocket to bring out the bottle of pills.

Andy sat still. He felt battered.

"You see," Hep began, "how the lust for gold—"

"I don't want to think about gold!"

"Then why not get out?" Hep put it to him softly.

Why not? Andy almost said it aloud. But he knew why not. Aside from a selfish reluctance to leave his father, there were the others to think of. He couldn't just go off and live in some pleasant, sheltered place, well fed and comfortable, while the rest of them struggled under the looming shadow of the crusher. Even though it worked a hardship on his father, Andy knew he had to stay and see this business through.

"I can't go yet," he said quietly, hoping that someday his father would understand.

"My boy, my boy! You're far too young to know what you're giving up. Think about it—I won't write them for a while—" And then Hep broke off as they heard voices at the front of the house. First Will Brett, speaking faster than usual. Then Misery let out a whoop.

"Everybody! Out to the kitchen! Hurry up!" he yelled happily. "Remi, Josey, come on down here. Come on, you fellers—" he charged through the dining room, waving to Hep and Andy. Close on his heels Brett came —hadn't even stopped to wash up. Trickles of perspiration had made channels down the dust on his face and he was carrying an armful of rock. Wordlessly he tossed Andy a chunk, another to Hep—he was hardly able to keep from grinning. And yet when Andy examined his it didn't look like much; fine-grained dark gray stone slashed with streaks of dull, leaden-colored metal.

Out in the kitchen Misery had caught Adeline around the waist and waltzed her over to the stove, where he took off one of the stove lids and laid a chunk of the ore right on the hot coals.

"Hee, hee, hee," he chortled, "askin' me how far we gonna dig the drift, what-for do I wanta start her here and not there. Hee, hee, hee! Bill, you tell 'em."

Brett glanced around—the whole group had gathered about the stove by now. "That first day when we looked over the mine, I found a piece of float just up the hill from the shaft. Calaverite, like this. I thought the vein must be somewhere near, but I didn't want to get everybody's hopes up too early. Besides, if the town had got wind of it, we'd have had half the district scrabbling around all over the hill, looking for the apex. So I only told Misery."

"Float?" Remi fingered the rock. "I do not know of this."

"That's a chip off the vein, buster." Misery was hopping around on one foot and the other. "Yes-sir-ree!"

"When a vein emerges on the surface of the ground," Brett explained, "some pieces always break off. Eventually they get washed down by the weather to some resting place nearby. When you find float, you know a vein has apexed somewhere above. The piece I found was at the bottom of the rise just behind the mine, so I figured there might be good pay-rock somewhere in the depths of the hill. When we got to working the crosscut, Misery found evidence of a rift in the structure of the rock, and we decided to chance it. We dug out toward the spot where I made the find. And last night the powder laid bare a whole streak of this. It isn't the vein itself, but I think we've run into a pretty good offshoot."

"But what is it?" Andy asked, eying the dull slashes of metal with some disappointment. He had heard there was lead in some of the ore, but the idea of mining it didn't appeal to him.

"You want to know what that is?" Misery dug an elbow in his ribs. "Look." The rock on the coals was red-hot now. As they watched, the surface seemed to come alive, metal bubbling out of it to stand in tiny beads—shimmering, glistening, bright drops of molten gold. "That's high-grade ore, skipper. I'd say she'll run five hundred dollars the ton or more. Ladies and gents, the old *Sidewinder* has struck! I think we all just got rich."

PART III
BLACK POWDER

Seventeen

That first pay day, as Andy headed for town with thirty dollars in his Levis, he knew he should have felt on top of the world. Everybody else seemed to. The streets were teeming with a Saturday-afternoon crowd, all with money in their pockets and zest in their faces. They moseyed along in bunches or in pairs. Nobody seemed to be alone that golden July afternoon.

Even the people back at the house had been caught up in a rare moment of comradeship when Remi had handed out their shares just now. Eyes aglint with private speculations, they had laughed together, joshing about the *Sidewinder* and its lucky "bite." Only Will Brett had taken his money and gone on off upstairs, his absence hardly noticed. For a while Andy had hung around, trying to get into the spirit, for there was plenty to celebrate.

After two weeks of hard work the ore shoot had

yielded enough to settle all debts, pay what they owed on the lease, and invest in a few new tools. Misery had been repaid for their board and back rent and there were still a few hundred dollars left over to divide.

Andy had been stunned to have three ten-dollar bills thrust into his hand—more cash than he'd ever had at one time in his life. But strangely it didn't bring him much pleasure. Now as he wandered into the heart of town, he felt like a stranger to these happy crowds. Almost as if he had already left them and was looking back from a long distance.

Feeling mixed up and uneasy, he stopped in front of a hardware store window; pretended to be studying a display of blacksmith tools. Secretly he was eying his own reflection in the glass, wondering what was the matter with him.

The face that looked back at him was older than it had been a couple of months ago. The dark hair fell loose over his forehead, shadowing troubled eyes. Kind of a rawboned, awkward, lanky picture he presented, Andy thought critically. Must have grown a couple of inches—coat was getting short in the sleeves and tight in the shoulders. Pretty faded shirt—made him look like a country rube. The face in the window tightened with defiance; nothing wrong with farmer-style clothes.

But they wouldn't do to go East in—he knew that. He wasn't even sure what people did wear in Virginia. He supposed he should have asked Hep, but the truth was, his uncle had been put out with him ever since their discussion that first day the letter had come. He seemed hurt, to have his help refused. And Andy knew it was going to be difficult to explain why he was almost ready now to change his mind.

He wasn't even certain himself; it was just a feeling that had grown on him steadily. Ever since the strike had been made, he could see he wasn't needed here any more. No reason to have a guilty conscience about leaving them all. They were busy—so intent on the work that they had no time for bickering. In fact they were going at it so hard they kept shunting him aside.

He had to admit he really wasn't much help down the shaft. He even could see why, at times, he was in the way. And at home Adeline was downright impatient, shooing him out of the kitchen so that she could work faster. Every day now she made a hot lunch to take up to the men at noon. They were starting to work at sunup these days and she said they needed plenty of good food. Even Josey was helping out with a prickly sort of enthusiasm. It was nice to have everybody pulling together, but the hustle had left Andy adrift. And the more he thought, the more he had to admit the inevitable fact that he was still undoubtedly a burden on his father.

Even though the mine was paying off well now, this pick-and-shovel work was a hard life for a man to lead. Will Brett's lean frame had lost flesh and his face was gaunt. So tired that he fell asleep in a chair on the front porch these evenings. His hands, which had been so handsomely groomed once, were wiry-tough now, and when he slept they twitched with weariness. Andy had sat in the dusk of the porch, night after night, and thought about it.

Unlike the others, his father wasn't taking joy in their good luck. After his first flare of satisfaction over the strike he had suddenly withdrawn again into that unreadable intentness. Went about his work as if bent on making the most of it, but hardly with much relish. Andy got the uncomfortable feeling that if it weren't for him, his father would have pulled stakes and quit.

It preyed on his mind these nights as he lay awake and wondered what to do. For the truth was, the idea of going off to live in Virginia made a sick emptiness inside him. No matter how kind the old people were or what comforts they might offer, there could be no real belonging. It would never be his own home, any more than Grandpa's store was. Older folk are too far ahead in years. Only his father could ever be his real family.

He didn't know how long he had stood there, looking blindly into the window, when he roused to find someone standing next to him. As he looked up in slow surprise, Will Brett smiled a little. He had spruced up. Fresh-shaven and well pressed in his gambler's clothes, the flat-crowned hat set slightly aslant over his dark eyes, he was a different man from the dusty digger who trudged home so wearily these nights. There was something about him, too, that was a cut above the others who strode along the streets of Victor. Andy hadn't noticed it before, but there was a finer edge on his father's look, a dignity in the way he held himself. A

146

man that a son could be proud of, if there hadn't been this wall of mystery between them.

It was on the tip of his tongue to just come right out with it. Say, *howdy, Father, I'm glad you came along. Let's walk somewhere and talk.* But in the lengthening silence, Brett's smile had withdrawn just slightly, and his tone was a bit bluff as he spoke.

"Well, boy, are you going to take up smithing next? You've been looking at those tools for at least ten minutes."

The moment of closeness vanished. Andy felt hot and foolish. "No, sir, I was just thinking—of buying a pick," he said for no reason.

"Is that still on your mind—that I haven't let you bust rock?" Brett clapped him on the shoulder, his hand tightened, and Andy almost winced under the strength of that grip. "You're building good muscle, but as long as your bones are growing so fast, I don't want you to strain yourself. Anyhow, tools are general expense. You should be looking for something better to spend that hard-earned cash on. Come along, let's see what the town has to offer."

As they started down the street together Andy felt even more ill at ease. He was painfully conscious that beside his father's well-tailored attire he looked dowdier than ever. Heading for the first mercantile store he could spot, he muttered an explanation.

"I've got to buy some clothes. These are pretty old."

"I was going to suggest that," his father said lightly,

not at all unkindly, but the embarrassment grew in Andy. His father must have despised these shabby garments for quite a while.

As they browsed around the clothing store it was easy to see that Brett was an expert, choosing the best quality —such as Andy would never have dared pick for himself. To pay for these, thirty dollars was not going to be enough. Hesitantly he suggested some less expensive things, but his father shook his head.

"Cheap clothes are a poor investment. Don't worry about the price—that's my responsibility."

It was nice of him, but the last word piled more guilt on Andy's uneasy conscience. He just couldn't take favors from his father and then go kiting off to Virginia. Helplessly he cast about for a way to break the news, until at last Brett noticed that he wasn't taking much part in the shopping.

"Confound it, I suppose I've been too insistent again. I always seem to manage to put your back up," he said, half joking. "What ails you, boy? Are you still wary of my money? Surely this that I was paid today isn't 'dirty.' It was earned by what is commonly called 'honest sweat.' "

"Yes, sir," Andy agreed hurriedly. "It's not that."

"Then what? Am I forcing some apparel on you that you don't like? I admit I don't know much about what boys want."

"I want—to talk to you." Andy almost strangled on it.

His father stood hesitant a minute, then nodded.

"Suppose we find a more relaxed atmosphere to do it in?" Leading the way out of the store, he scanned the street and headed for an ice-cream parlor down at the corner. Cool inside, almost deserted, it was sweet with aromas. When the clerk had drawn their sarsaparilla and retired, they were all alone at the high marble counter.

"It's too bad we've not had the chance to do this before," Brett said almost shyly, "but, as you're beginning to see, a gold mine is a slave driver."

"Yes, sir. I've been thinking about that. I didn't know it was going to take so long or be so hard on—everybody. And I know you'd probably like to move on, with Duke snooping around and all. Maybe your life's in danger."

"Safety's never been a particular goal of mine." His father seemed puzzled. "What's on your mind?"

"Well, it's just that I'm kind of making it hard on you, and I'm not much help down the shaft. So I've been thinking I ought to tell Uncle Hep that I'll go. To Virginia, I mean. He wrote them and they said they want me."

Some furious emotion struck lightning-swift across Brett's face and was gone again, leaving his expression as blank as it had been the night at the stage station, with a shotgun rammed into his back. After a minute he said coldly, "And what the devil's business is it of Hep's, to arrange for your future? Or to advise the family about you at all?"

"Don't be angry at him—he was just doing it for your good. He said they'd send me to school, and he told me how you never cared much for all that. So if I went, it would save you a lot of bother."

"Sounds as though he's been most persuasive. His zeal is something to be thought about. It isn't the first time he's shown acute solicitude for your welfare. Before you arrived—after our trouble in Black Hawk—he used all his reasoning on me; told me I'd be putting you in danger to let you come with us. I happened to feel it was worth the risk, myself. But, of course, you may have a different opinion. You must consider your best interests. Schooling, eh? What did he tell you about me and college?"

"Just said you didn't want to go."

"That's not the entire truth. I attended for a while. Left for lack of money. Your worthy grandparents are generous to the core, so long as you comply with their standards of what's fitting for a Virginia gentleman. My peculiar ambition didn't, so they cut off my funds. Which was their perfect right. I only tell you this so that you'll be aware of the problems as well as the advantages in this offer of theirs."

"What was it you wanted to be?" Andy asked curiously.

"Well, it was *not* my desire to become an attorney. That's what they had chosen for me." He laughed curtly. "Though I must admit that my few law studies have stood me in good stead—behind the poker table." Having finished his drink, he sat flipping the penny in that restless way of his.

"Do you miss gambling a lot?" Andy ventured.

"Like a man misses a disease. You get so used to it, you don't know how to act normally when you're relieved of it. Everything I say turns out to sound like a bet: 'Call and raise you ten.' Even Misery has accused me of wearing a 'poker' face. Or maybe you've already observed that, yourself. It may even account for these sudden daydreams of yours about getting out of here and going to Virginia." He shrugged—an odd, hopeless little gesture. "At any rate give me the experience, just this once, of being normal and fatherly. I want to buy you those clothes."

Neither of them spoke again as they went back outside, moving along the street under the hot afternoon sun, jostled by the crowd, surrounded by the laughter and chatter of happy shoppers. Somehow Andy felt more depressed than ever.

At last his father went on, following some inner train of thought. "The Bretts are fine people—they have more wealth than several gold mines, so you'd not be sacrificing in that respect, if you went to them. As for shaping yourself to fit their image, you might find it becomes you. Some people are naturally born to be aristocratic. Never mind how I feel about it. I can't offer you a better life"—it was wrung out of him painfully—"at least, not yet. I've thought— But then I don't trade in vague promises. All I can say is that if you decide to go, I won't stand in your way. But before you make up your mind, I've a favor to ask of you."

It brought a return of warmth, rising slowly in Andy. "Yes, sir—anything!"

"You've wanted from the beginning to know more about gold. If I've seemed scornful, it's because I forget at times that I had to learn its various values myself. There's a certain importance in knowing just how it gets wrenched from the earth—at what sacrifice. Something you'll never forget—it may even give you a perspective on the other riches of life. That's why I let you come down into the mine. But your education isn't quite complete. You're only aware of part of the struggle. I've shown you some use of tools, and Misery has explained some basic facts about rock. Remi is a walking lesson in the arithmetic of the business. But you've still to feel the blast that comes when black powder explodes and the ore crashes. Since you and your uncle are on such confidential terms, I'm sure he won't mind if you spend the next two weeks with him below ground. Only every other night, of course. I want you to watch him handle a drill, see the care he takes with powder—he's a good craftsman. I don't want you to try to do any of it yourself, but to get the feel of it. Will two weeks longer in these parts be intolerable?"

"No, sir."

Brett's troubled look eased into a sort of dry humor. "You think that's an odd request—your face is as fluent as mine is frozen. Never mind. There's so much now that you don't understand about me, one more peculiarity can't hurt much."

Eighteen

"There's something afoot! That's plain enough!" Hep muttered darkly. For all his weariness this news had jarred him wide-awake. "What ridiculous game is Billy playing, expecting a mere boy to learn the dangerous art of black powder?"

"He just wants me to watch how you do it," Andy said apologetically. "I'll try not to get in your way."

"I can show you the whole process in one night, if it's of any interest—which I imagine it is not. I tell you he's got some devious reason that he's not letting on."

"Well, I reckon maybe he wants to give me time to think some more before I make up my mind to go to Virginia." Andy tried to sound regretful, but the truth was, he secretly felt gratified. Maybe at the end of the two weeks he and his father would have another talk and inch a little nearer each other.

"So, you've told him about my writing home." Hep sighed. "And I suppose he resented my putting a finger in the pie. But I'd be less than human if I didn't try to save you from such a fate as this." Hep glanced down at his sweat-stained clothes and scuffed boots. He had not yet been to bed though it was eight o'clock in the morning.

A few minutes earlier Andy, lying awake in the next room, had heard him climb the stairs. Still in his night-shirt he had gone to greet his uncle and break the news of his father's request. Now as they sat side by side on one of the beds, Hep was coughing, a dry, insistent cough.

"It's unhealthy down there. Powder smoke. No sleep. He wants a growing boy to stay up till all hours—"

"But you usually set your shots off by ten or eleven o'clock at night, don't you?" Andy had been privately wondering at the lateness of his uncle's return.

"True enough. The reason that I was so long getting home this morning was that when I came up out of the shaft last night I thought I glimpsed a skulker below on the hillside. Nothing to do but stand watch until the morning shift arrived."

It was one of their worries, the possibility of theft. For there was one small section of the ore which was richer than the rest—Misery said it was made to order for high-grading. That was why they hadn't yet hired any extra help with the digging; why all of them had kept the strike a secret. And yet someone could have found out—maybe through the freight teamster. And if they ever located that half-hidden ventilator shaft, it would be a matter then of just climbing down the ladders. It worried Andy to think of it.

"Did you get a good look at him?"

"No, nothing came of it. But"—Hep rubbed his eyes wearily—"it's a burden, lad, gold is. You think all problems will be solved by the finding of it, but I can assure you they are just beginning. It's a headache, a headache."

Andy laughed a little. "I've just been thinking it must be a pretty good thing to have it around, after all. Everybody's happy now."

"You think so, lad?" Hep coughed some more. "Well, well, you're young. Keep your illusions. Get out of this place quickly before you become cynical."

They were interrupted by a sharp rap at the door. It was Adeline. "Andy?"

"Yes'm."

"Get dressed up. Your pa told me to take you to church this morning. Hurry on now." Her heels click-clicked away down the hall.

Hep smiled gloomily. "Now we have the ultimate hypocrisy—church. By order of Billy Brett, who hasn't been inside such an institution in years. Well, they say the biggest sinners sit in the front pews and sing loudest. Excuse me, lad, I didn't mean to say that of your father. But if you do decide to make your escape, remember I can arrange for you to be on your way in a matter of hours."

The church services had made Andy homesick. They had sung "Bringing in the Sheaves"—always a favorite hymn of Grandma's. He was thinking how pleased she'd have been with the way he looked in this new dark-blue broadcloth suit. Whatever else Will Brett may not have known about boys, he understood one thing: Andy had outgrown the old overalls in more ways than one. The new clothes made him look older.

Adeline noticed it too. She walked along beside him with her arm hooked through his elbow as if he were a grown man. But then this business of going to church had shaken her up in some way he couldn't comprehend. She seemed to want to cling to him—he had never seen her so nervous. Now she was talking to herself in a hushed whisper; he could just catch the words.

". . . shouldn't have let him talk me into it."

"You upset about something?" Andy asked with brotherly bluntness.

"I was just wondering what your pa had in his head, to talk me into a thing like this. Oh, I reckon he meant it kindly—said I ought to get out of the house once in a while. Maybe he thought both you and me needed a little sermonizing. Being a man, he couldn't know what he was getting me into, sending me to rub elbows with all those hoighty ladies." She was walking faster, as if the thought goaded her—her heels were banging down hard on the boardwalk.

"I thought we got along all right."

"You did fine. Holding my coat so polite—somewhere along the way you've had good raising."

"About the same as yours, I'll bet. My grandpa had a store near Wheatly. That's where I grew up."

"Where?"

"That's in Kansas. North of Abilene. Just a little place—it isn't even on a railroad."

"Kansas? Honest? I'm from Wichita!" For a minute her brown eyes brightened. It occurred to Andy that she was looking better these days. Walking back and forth from the mine had brought out freckles on her nose and color in her cheeks. "Kansas was a good place to live. I used to think it was boring, but it was just decent and quiet. I sure miss it sometimes, but"—she shrugged—"you don't look back."

"I do," Andy admitted. "I can't help thinking about it once in a while. I'd sure like to see my grandpa again. And there were some pretty good animals lived around the place. Of course, they're all gone off now."

"My folks are gone, too. Moved East somewhere. I don't even know where they are." She laughed shortly. "They disowned me when I got the notion to come out here. I don't blame 'em—I was crazy. Young girls are, mostly. I read in the papers how everybody was getting rich. I don't know—you dream about meeting some handsome miner—"

"You still might."

She shook her head. "After all I've seen of men I know what kind of women they marry. Those ladies back there in church—those *nice* females with the turned-up snoots. Looking at me like I might start dancing the Mule Skinner's Delight any minute. Gosh-almighty, what do they want? I dress as plain as I know how." She frowned down at her clothes.

So that was why she wore those drab brownish things. Andy struggled to understand the problems that a woman must have.

"I reckon it's my hair," she was muttering, "but I can't do anything about that."

Andy was sorry to hear it. He'd been hoping maybe she could. Grandma had once mentioned that some women dye their hair, and he had supposed this must be what made Adeline's such an awful color. Even though she kept her bonnet pulled down over it as far as possible—and at home she always wore a dust cap around the house—it still showed in bright orange curls along the collar of her dress and over her forehead. But if it was just naturally that shade nobody could blame her.

"I don't know about those women," he said earnestly, "but I don't think a man would hold it against you."

She gave him a bitter smile. "You're a nice kid. I wish you didn't have to grow up. Never mind, I'm doing all right—earning gold of my own. I don't have to ask anybody for a cent!"

"You think that's going to—sort of—fix everything up for you? The gold?" Andy was thinking of Hep's ominous predictions.

"If you mean, will it make those biddies invite me to join their sewing circle—it won't. Of course, I could make 'em take notice, them and their cold hearts. They deserve it! Wouldn't they curl if they were to find their men stepping out, of a night, down to my dance hall?" Her young face settled into its old toughness and she smiled. "The fellows would come, too. I know how to get 'em—have the handsomest girls in town, high-class girls. I'd pay 'em well—twenty cents, maybe even two-bits a dance. And the men would come through with it, too. Got to have a good piano player—I could get Jimmy Fingers, he's the best. Serve refreshments—no cheap stuff either. You know what I'll have? One of those big ceiling lights with about a million candles in it, and all dripping with glass. I'll have the handsomest place in town—run the Single-Jill smack out of business!"

As she talked along fiercely it didn't sound to Andy as though she were taking much real pleasure in the idea. And considering what he had seen of the dance hall it worried him to think of her planning to go back to such a life. Uneasily he wondered what the others might be going to do with their share of the profits. He hated to face the fact that Hep might have been right.

When they reached the house and he saw Remi seated on the front porch, glued to his account books as usual, Andy got the sudden notion to find out. While Adeline went on inside he lingered on the porch, hitched a hip over the railing, and let his foot dangle as he waited for the Frenchman to finish adding a column of figures. The total brought a smile to Remi's delicate, sensitive mouth—a smile that broadened as he looked up at Andy.

"Everything is well, eh, young Andrew? I see the new clothes. Very good."

"Yes, sir. It's a help to have a little cash again. I don't know why Uncle Hep seemed to think it was going to give us all a lot of problems."

"Problems? Of course." Remi shrugged. "But there are worse kinds of a problem than to be rich, especially in this country of yours where people measure only by the dollar and not by a man's nobility."

"You mean in France they admire you because you're a duke or a prince or something?"

Remi laughed. "No, no, I do not mean that. I mean nobility of spirit—a gracious manner of living, a dignity. You see? Well, soon I shall demonstrate. When there is enough money saved I shall build a château up on the hillside above this ugly town. The money-grubbers in the streets below will look up at it and witness for once something of gentility."

"You're going to build a—what was it?"

"Château—you would call it a 'castle,' but that is not really correct. A great mansion, then, of grandeur and stateliness. A place of beauty. There will be gardens, fountains, tall stone walls—I shall import the stones from France."

"Why?" Andy asked, mystified. With all the rock around—?

But Remi misunderstood the question. "One needs walls to maintain a privacy. With wealth, one can afford to be discriminating. Only the upper class will come within my gates."

"And you'll live there—just you and Josey?"

"Someday I will have sons. When they look around them at the place I have provided, they will be proud." Gathering up his account books, he added, "I must go in now. If you will excuse me—?" That was one thing about Remi—he certainly was polite. If that was part of this nobility, it was probably a good thing. But a French castle—in Cripple Creek? With only the best people allowed inside?

"That lets me out," Andy remarked under his breath.

The words brought a little titter from the hammock. Glancing around, he saw Josey, so deep in its folds he hadn't noticed her. She had on a new dress, filmy white like a little princess, and her hair was looped up on top of her head, tied with a pink velvet ribbon. More nobility at work, Andy thought—she looked like sugar and cream. Then she giggled again.

"If you wear such el-e-gant attire all the time, little Andrew, we may invite you to our château to have wine with us. Lovely, white wine . . ."

"I guess you're going to spend your share of the gold on food and drink." Andy grinned.

Josey brushed the thought aside with an airy gesture. "We will have a French chef, of course—Remi will attend to that. I have other plans for my money. Truly *marvelous* plans. Such as the way I shall reward the gentleman who owns a certain rathole where we once were forced to live, with the vermin, in the basement."

"You're going to do him some favor?" Andy thought there was a dangerous glint in her look.

"Ah, but yes, a favor indeed. I shall ruin him. The details will not be difficult—he wasn't rich, not so rich as I shall be. Then when he is pleading on his knees for an extension of the mortgage I will—what is the word? —foreclose this old house and blow it up with a nice little piece of dynamite. Perhaps I shall be kind enough to give the wretch employment—he can sweep our wine cellar. But he must stay down there, always, where it is dark." She smiled dreamily. "And then there is the grocery gentleman."

"You've got plans for him?" Andy was on the verge of laughing, but somehow he had an idea she didn't intend to be funny.

"A lovely scoundrel—I will buy his store, and then I will buy all the other stores around. And to him I will sell not one morsel of food except—beans. He shall have nothing but beans to eat the rest of his whole life. He will eat them or perish!"

"That's going to take a lot of money."

"I do not care if it takes all I have, I shall get my revenge!" she said between clenched teeth, her eyes very wide and almost blank of expression as she looked off into an imaginary future.

Uneasily Andy said, "Well, if—if you'll excuse me—"

But she seemed not to notice as he let himself into the house.

The confusion in him was growing fit to bust. He felt as if he just had to ask somebody about this. And the only person who would really understand was Misery. He'd been through it all before—had seen his own sons go bad and the town turn sour on him. Of all of them he would still have his wits about him.

He found the old man dozing out on the back stoop— at least he looked half asleep, tipped back in the straight kitchen chair with his battered old hat down over his eyes. But when Andy hesitated to rouse him he looked up keenly.

"There y'are, skipper. Set down, if y' kin find a place around that's clean enough to park them fancy duds of yours. I was just figgerin' a batch of calculations. Mebbe you can help. What's seven into twenty thousand dollars?"

"Make it twenty-one thousand and I can do it."

"Oh, shore, a thousand or two don't make no difference. Comes out three thousand apiece, don't it? Supposin' each of us puts that much out of our share back into the business—that'll buy a lot of steam. Pneumatic drills we got to have. Got to enlarge the shaft, set up ore bins, lay track down to the nearest spur. We got to do away with the wagon freight—mules ain't no way to haul a whole lot of ore."

"Is there going to be a lot?"

"Shucks, yes. Next week I'll open two or three new

drifts. No reason to suppose there ain't more and richer rock right around the corner so to speak. Next year, 'stead of figgerin' thousands we'll figger hundred thousands, maybe a million. Divvied up seven ways? That'll be the ticket, eh, skipper?"

"Do we need that much?"

But the old man didn't seem to hear. "Mebbe I'll put *all* my share back into the hole. You got to treat your mine good if you want her to pay off. Can't do better than invest your profits back. There's one thing to remember about gold—you got to use her right or she's a buckin' witch. Spend her wrong and you'll jinx your luck."

"Yes, sir," Andy said, "but you had so much money before. You still do—"

"Talkin' about luck," Misery was going on, "I'd say you're the one brought us ours, skipper. If it wasn't for you, none of this would've come to pass. We wouldn't have no mine or be all familied up together. Everybody set to make a fortune—your folks, Addie, Remi, even that little she-devil girl. They got you to thank for this."

But Andy was thinking dismally that he should have taken the old story more seriously. First the potato—ruined. Now a house full of people clenched in a feverish partnership for no good purpose.

"Yes-sir-ree," Misery marveled, "you got an odd kind of luck—what you might call a—a—"

Andy said it for him, silently, sick at heart. What you might call a—"golden touch."

Nineteen

In those next days a change seemed to come over the household—at first as subtle as a thin veil of high cloud, dimming the sunlight just a little. The members of the family all got very polite to each other, but at the same time a strange wariness came in their manner, as if they were waiting for something, listening. . . .

Andy himself was nervous as a quaking aspen. Like the silvery leaves on the trees, his misgivings fluttered inside him at every least breath of ill wind—each secret look that anyone cast, every suppressed remark. They were all breaking off words, holding back things they'd been about to say. He tried to put a finger on just what was happening.

Plenty of time to think, these evenings below ground with Hep. Once down the shaft his uncle became edgy and strange. He had told Andy that very first night to find some place back out of the way and make himself comfortable. That was all. For hours there had been nothing to do but watch him drill holes with an unrelenting haste that didn't permit much talk. Under the flickering light of the candles spiked into the walls, the bit seemed alive in his hands, twisting around and around, biting deeper and deeper into the hard rock. When one hole was done he would start another, making five or six in all, spaced evenly up and down and across the face of the drift.

Finally, on this third work night, Andy dared ask a question. "Why do you have to have so many? Couldn't you just make one big one in the middle, instead?"

Hep jumped, as if he'd forgotten Andy's presence. "Ah, yes, we're supposed to be teaching you about explosives, aren't we?" He sounded impatient, but made an effort at his usual jocularity. "By now you're probably aware that it's devilish tedious work, but there is a science to it, nephew. It isn't every man who can drive a tunnel clean as this one. It's not just the number of shots, though you'd soon see that one large one wouldn't bring down as much ore as a number of lesser ones. The big secret, though—I give it to you free of charge, my boy—is in the angle at which the holes are drilled. In the present instance these are pointed at the heart of the ore shoot, so that the blast will focus inward. Let it explode out or up, and you'll crack the walls of the tunnel. That means timbering, loose rock, a number of unpleasant possibilities. There, now, you can tell your father you know all about black powder."

The edge on the words and the irritation with which he turned back to his work made Andy swallow his other questions and sit silent. He was thinking it was a far cry from that day on the stream when Hep had seemed to enjoy explaining things. He had been happy enough then. Now he was grim, going at the work with dogged distaste. It was plain to see that he had no faith in the "touch."

Andy fidgeted and worried. That was where his thoughts always wound up these days. He kept thinking of the "golden touch" and of his teacher. She was a tenderhearted person—certainly never would have wanted to wish some curse on him. In fact she only said it because she was so grateful that her bird was all right.

The whole scene came back to him—the pretty little yellow bird hunched down in the corner, looking grim, and the teacher making knots in her handkerchief. She'd heard that Andy had good luck with his own menagerie and had asked him to try to doctor the bird. It had looked to him as though the canary was in moulting season; it had lost its tail feathers and seemed embarrassed and frowsy. Probably just low in spirit. Recalling that when Grandpa felt poorly he always put red pepper in his coffee, Andy had doused some hard-boiled egg with a little cayenne and shoved it in the cage. When that little bird took its first nibble you could almost see the warmth spread through its innards. In half an hour it was back upon its perch.

Teacher had gone all to pieces. "The way you know how to treat these little creatures, you have a real touch

—a golden touch!" That's exactly what she had said. Later on, when Andy had the chance to ask her, she'd told where the expression came from—the story of the old king. He could see now that he had lost her original meaning by concentrating so hard on the thought of finding gold. And all along it was only his way with animals—a harmless sort of knack—that had set off a whole wrong idea about his luck.

He felt pretty foolish. And worst of all the discovery came too late to do much good. Through his thickheadedness he had got a lot of people in a spot that wasn't likely to bring them much happiness. And people were not like animals, not by a long shot. People, he had never understood and probably never would.

Take Hep, there. Finished drilling now, he was bending over a keg of powder, swearing at it under his breath when the lid didn't come off easily. Why did he lose all his droll good humor when he came down here? It didn't make sense—though, come to think of it, Andy had seen the same thing happen to the raccoon. It was usually gentle and clownish all day, but when night came on it liked to roam the store, slipping off in spite of his efforts to keep it in the loft. Once Andy had caught it in the act of opening a box of cookies—it could pry the top off almost anything with those little hands. When he had come up, it had looked over its shoulder at him blackly, ready to bite.

The memory made him uneasy, and he told himself again, sternly, that people should not be compared with animals. Getting up, he strolled over to his uncle's side.

"Can I help you with that, sir?"

"No, no, I've got it now." Hep had the lid off and scooped out a measure of black powder. Andy picked some up in his palm—innocent-looking stuff, hard black grains of irregular sizes. He watched Hep tamp it into the holes, little by little, until each one was full. Then into the tight-packed powder he began to insert the caps.

Andy picked one out of the box—a thin cylinder like a small firecracker. He had seen Hep clinch the metal end to a length of fuse with a neat little tool like a pair of pliers. Searching around, he found it.

"Can I put fuses on these for you?"

"Good heavens, no!" Hep turned and took them from him. "You could blow us both to kingdom come! The charge in these caps is highly sensitive—many a man's had his hands blown off crimping a fuse carelessly. Now stand back, nephew, and don't play with these materials. They're not toys."

Sheepishly Andy stepped aside and watched while Hep finished setting the caps, then packed the open ends of the holes with mud made of moistened rock dust. This was to keep the blast from emptying backward into the tunnel—that much Andy could guess. Finally all that was left showing were the ends of the fuses, hanging like little bits of old brown string down the face of the rock. Each was a slightly different length so that the charges would go off one at a time, loosening more rock for the next to bring down. Winding the ends together, Hep connected them all to a length of larger fuse.

"You can pick things up now," he said. Andy helped him carry their equipment out of the drift. Then Hep began to unroll the large fuse carefully, walking backward, making sure there were no breaks or kinks in it. When it came to this point both he and Andy moved carefully, without speaking, as though the merest word might touch off the mighty charge that had been set.

Coming to the tip of the fuse, Hep bent and touched his candle to the end. Instantly the stringlike cord began to sputter and burn, sparks eating up the fuse rapidly, racing along the floor of rock—Andy could hardly tear his eyes from it.

"Care to wait there until she goes off?" Hep asked as he walked off into the main tunnel. Hastily Andy followed. At the foot of the ventilator shaft they paused and stood silent. This was the hardest part—waiting, not daring to make a sound. For Hep was listening. With his head cocked he stood taut. At last it came—an earsplitting roar that shook the rock underfoot. Bracing hard, Andy tried to hear what Hep heard—the separate detonations as each shot exploded, for they were only a second apart. He thought they all fired, but he wasn't sure.

"Did that get 'em all?" he asked in a hushed voice.

His uncle nodded. "Shall we get on home?" Powder smoke was beginning to eddy out of the drift and circulate into the tunnel behind them as they started up the ladder.

Every time they made the climb up this narrow little hole it seemed longer to Andy. Rock so close around him he couldn't bend his knees naturally or his backside would scrape. Below him, Hep was puffing along, coughing—his cough seemed to be getting worse. Though it was drafty and cold, Andy's shirt was clinging wetly by the time they scrambled out into the fresh night air. The moon was up, laying a white sheen over the sleeping valley. As they stood there catching their breath, Andy ventured another question.

"Suppose one of the charges hadn't gone off—what would you do?"

"Have to pull it out, come tomorrow morning, unless you want to add to the population of heaven." His uncle seemed to regain some of that jovial spirit. As they started home he was going on in a brisk voice. "Honestly, nephew, haven't you come to the conclusion that it's pointless for you to spend any more time down there? I've shown you all there is to see. Why not reason with your father about discontinuing this dangerous business? Frankly, the responsibility for your safety is making me quite upset."

And it dawned on Andy that it probably was, indeed, the cause of his uncle's uneasy behavior down below. He could also agree that he wasn't doing much good. But some feeling lingered—that Will Brett never asked a thing without a purpose. Reluctantly he said, "I'm sorry you're worried for me, Uncle Hep. But I reckon I'd better do as Father asks. It isn't for much longer."

"Yes, yes," Hep muttered. "Not—much—longer."

Andy yawned and followed along, scuffing down the road wearily. He was thinking of bed, when something suddenly jolted him wide-awake. He couldn't tell whether it was some faint sound or a movement in the bushes, but he was sure someone else was around. Pausing, he pretended to tie his shoe while Hep walked on ahead. As he crouched there, all his senses ajar, he was certain of it. The back of his neck went prickly as he stood up and walked on down the path.

They hadn't yet reached the foot of the hill where their private property connected to the main road into town. So whoever was up there could only be interested in the *Sidewinder*. And if the curiosity was honest, why lurk in the shadows? Drowsiness vanished, Andy determined to get back there somehow and take a look at the person. Though how to get away from his uncle—?

Luck was with him there. When they reached the main road, instead of turning toward home Hep paused. "Much as I dislike to leave you at this hour of night, nephew, the fact is I've got to go into Victor for a while. This afternoon I heard some news—of an old acquaintance who may have been seen around town. I must check on it without delay. Do you suppose you'll be able to make your way to the house safely?"

"Yes, sir. It's not far," Andy assured him fervently.

"I'll be all right." He pretended to start off along the way toward home, walking slowly. As soon as his uncle was out of sight he doubled back. His pulse was starting to pump as he made his way softly up the hillside.

He had walked over it so often he knew where the rock outcroppings were and was able to move quietly, without the scratch of dirt underfoot. When he came abreast of the place where he thought he'd heard someone, he stopped. In a moment he located it—a slightly rustling of clothes. And then in the moon shadows he made out a darker patch, hunched down behind a clutter of rock. It didn't look too big—not the silhouette of a man. As it moved slightly, moonlight touched a shock of blond hair. Andy's belly muscles relaxed and he grinned. Moving carefully until he was within a few feet, he lunged and grabbed.

"*Sacré bleu!*" she choked. Whirling, she set upon him in a flurry of fingernails and flying feet—kicking, scratching, until Andy let go and retreated.

"Josey, it's me!"

"*Ah, non!* You? You just went home!" she exclaimed softly.

Instinctively he kept his own voice low. "What the dickens are you up to, hiding out here?"

"Up to? I am up to killing somebody, *mon* Andrew! They are stealing our gold!"

"What in tarnation are you talking about?"

"You do not know? Ah, they will not tell us—they think we are children," she muttered furiously. "But I listen. Oh, I listen well! I hear Remi tell the old man: Last week there is not so much gold as there should be. And the old papa, he already knows this. I could tell— he did not yell at my brother as always. Maybe it is this old one who steals from us. That is what I must discover, so that I can inform the police and they will *hang him!*"

"You're imagining things—" he began, but she clutched his arm with fierce fingers.

"Haven't you felt it? How everyone is watchful now? There is a terrible *malaise* in the house. It is true! Someone is deceiving us all. I think perhaps it is the woman. She must know many men of this town—she has told one about our gold, perhaps."

"That's a lot of foolishment. You're going home," he said. "Right now. If there was anybody out here, he'd probably cut your throat. I could have, myself, before you even knew I was there. Go on, now, or I'll tell Remi."

She was about to protest when they heard a light sound that made them both freeze. It was close at hand —hard to tell from just which direction it came. Andy could feel Josey trembling.

Putting his lips close to her ear, he murmured almost soundlessly, "I'll find out who it is, but you must get out of here. Quick now!"

The sound came again, as if the man had moved a step nearer. Giving her a little shove, Andy started her on the way. She scuttled off into the shadows and was gone—he heard light steps running down the path. And

then he was alone with the unknown presence somewhere out in that moonlight.

This time he was the sitting duck himself. He would
have liked to take to his own heels, but he was afraid
whoever it was would follow Josey. Peering up at the
silent hillside, he knew that he must be clearly visible
to anyone there. The only thing to do was make a move
of his own before the other could work close enough to
jump him.

Boldly he called, "All right, come on out—I see you
there!"

And almost at his elbow someone gave a slight snort
of humor. "I like a man who'll try a bluff, but you're
looking in the wrong direction."

Andy swung around, laughing shakily. "Father! You
had me scared! I thought you were a high-grader."

"I've just been listening to Josey filling you with tales
of treachery, fraud, theft, and general hanky-panky."

"You don't think it's true, do you?"

"I don't think anybody's going to run off with any
loot tonight. That's the best-guarded gold this side of
the Denver Mint. Remi is hiding in the shaft house.
Misery's lurking near the ventilator—I don't think
Remi knows that. Neither of them saw me. I decided
my services weren't needed so I was just coming back
to collect the little mademoiselle—I saw her here earlier.
She shouldn't be mixed up in this, and neither should
you. Where's Hep?"

"He had to go to town to see about something."

"After this, stick with him. He has an extra sense for danger and a way of protecting himself. When you're down below, stay close to his side—don't go up and do any private investigating. Understand?"

"No, sir," Andy said honestly. "I don't. Is there really something going on? Somebody is trying to steal the gold?"

"All I have to go on is a hunch. The main thing is that I may have gotten you into something dangerous without meaning to. Will you do as I say, even without understanding?"

"Yes, sir. But—"

"Then let's get home. I don't want anything to happen to the little girl." He nudged Andy and they started off on a short cut across the hill that would get them to the road more quickly than by the path. When they came to a patch of open meadow bright with moonlight, Brett pulled Andy down and led the way, walking half-crouched along the shadow of some tall sage, until they reached the shelter of an old rock dump. Andy supposed he shouldn't question his father, but curiosity was boiling inside him.

"If Remi and Misery are up at the mine, who do you think might see us?"

Brett hesitated. When he answered he sounded worried. "I don't know. And I don't want to jump to any wrong conclusions. But one thing I believe I'd better tell you, so you'll at least know what cards are on the table."

"Yes, sir?"

"It's just that—there was someone else out taking a breath of air just now. Up on that hillside above the mine. He had swapped the white hat for a darker one, but I caught a glint of light off his star. Just to make sure, I worked up close enough to get a good look. And it was no mistake—we were joined tonight by our old friend, Duke, in person."

Twenty

The velvet ribbon was a good blue—real Kansas-jaybird blue. Andy hoped it would do the trick. The girls in the Ladies' Apparel Shop had sworn it was the right color for red hair; only women know such things. They hadn't even laughed at Andy for asking.

Now all he had to do was think of a way to give it to Adeline so she wouldn't suspect that he was trying to cheer up her spirit. He had an idea she would resent that. Such a strong, positive manner she was putting on these days—she didn't want anybody to think she might be privately hurt by the sneery attitude of all those town ladies. Andy thought the ribbon might help. It seemed to him that if she just brushed some of those little tight curls out and let her hair fall naturally with a pretty ribbon in it, people would forget what a dreadful color it was.

At any rate he was determined to try, and even though it was coming on suppertime when he got home, he decided not to wait. Out in the kitchen Adeline was rattling the pans around the stove in a scurry, stirring this, tasting that. Her hair was almost hidden under the kerchief she wore pulled tight over her head and knotted in back.

"I'm glad you're home," she said busily. "We need some more wood."

"All right, in a minute. I've got something for you."

She looked startled when he handed her the paper sack. "What's this?"

"Sort of a going-away present. I may be leaving for the East pretty soon. My grandparents want me to come stay with them."

"I hate to hear that." Then she blushed a little. "Maybe I shouldn't say so—it's probably good for you to get out of this place. But it'll be hard on your pa."

"It will?"

"He's a lonesome fellow—seems like he must have been alone for a long time." She opened the sack and drew forth the ribbon, holding it up, speechless. For an instant her brown eyes widened with pleasure, but it was gone just as quickly. She stared at him almost with suspicion. "Why did you pick—this?"

"I don't know." Andy squirmed. Red pepper was so much simpler. "I—thought it would look good. Go on, put it on, huh?"

She winced as if he'd made some terrible joke.

"You're a real sweet kid. Go on, get out of here before I start to bawl." Shoving the ribbon in her pocket, she turned away fast, clanging the lids on the stove. "Get me some wood, will you?"

Discouraged, he went on out to the back yard. So that was that. Just a crazy notion and it had made her feel worse. Shows you couldn't fool around with people as if they were canary birds or something. Feeling shucked off and mean, he began to split wood.

He was going at it with a vengeance when the men got home from work. As they grouped around the pump in the back yard, sluicing dust off themselves, he could almost feel the weight of unspoken suspicions hanging on the air. Wary and silent they soaped and took turns with the towel.

Andy moseyed over. "How'd it go today?"

"Mmmph." Misery tossed the towel aside and went on in.

Brett looked worried and preoccupied. "We had a hard day." There was discouragement in the way he climbed the steps.

"Did something happen?" Andy asked Remi who was the least dirty and always washed the most.

The Frenchman shook his head. "We received a report from the smelter—it was disappointing. But do not concern yourself, Andrew. Everything is all right." He didn't sound happy.

Andy decided to come out in the open with it. "Josey tells me you suspect there may be a little high-grading going on."

Remi looked startled. "I did not know that she was aware. I mean, she is mistaken, of course. Foolish child —such a grand imagination. I will have to have a word with her."

"Oh, no, sir! Please don't. I didn't mean to tell on her. I didn't take it very seriously, anyhow, so don't blame her. She's sad enough as it is."

"Sad?" The Frenchman said it as if he didn't know the meaning of the word. "Excuse me, but you are wrong. She is delirious with joy—we both are—to have success at last. Ah, it is magnificent!"

"Well, I think she misses your home in France. Did you know that she goes up to the attic and cries and listens to a music box."

"*Eh bien*, we will buy her a dozen music boxes soon. We will have our château—that will be her home then. Meanwhile, if you are concerned that she may be a trifle melancholy, why not remedy this, eh? Give her a small kiss, you know—I have no objection." He winked and went on inside, leaving Andy to absorb the shock of that appalling suggestion.

Supper was a moody session. Misery was taking his pills again—he offered them to the table at large, but nobody would join him. Adeline had cooked the roast too fast and it was tough. Josey remarked that in France corn on the cob was considered food for horses only. Remi wouldn't touch the tapioca pudding—Andy didn't like it much either. It seemed to stare at him out of the dish.

He was glad when the meal was over, hoping to get

a chance to talk to his father alone. But Brett said he was dead-tired and went off to bed. Restlessly Andy roamed into the front room where Misery sat, sunk in his big leather chair, pondering something. High-graders, probably, Andy supposed, for the old man's eyes were bleak and the gnarled hands were clamped hard on his knees.

Andy stretched out on his belly on the sofa, chin on his arms, accusing himself scornfully of having tried again to meddle with people and failed. Through the open doorway he could see Josey out in the front yard, swinging on the fence gate—a lonely little figure in the mellow sundown light. But kissing her? That was too much. Everything in him staggered at the thought. Besides, she was probably feeling better, all over those bad notions of hers about getting revenge. She'd be happy in this country, as Remi said—he ought to know, he was her brother.

"You said"—over his shoulder he eyed Misery—"you said the other day that gold's got to be spent right. Do you think it's a good idea to build a castle?"

The old man roused slightly. "Who's gonna do that?"

"Remi and Josey. It's going to be just like the ones in France, even with French stones. He's going to put it on the hill above Victor and only high-class people can come inside. Remi wants his sons to be proud."

Misery gave a sniff like a hound scenting a possum in a woodpile. "That's what he reckons, eh? I could tell him a few things about that. Sons—I know all about 'em.

Give 'em too much easy cash and they'll grow up expectin' more. No backbone, no respect, no git-up-and-git. I'd have done better to turn mine out with ten bucks apiece and tell 'em to go hunt their own gold. Do it the hard way, same as I did—that's where you get to feelin' proud."

"Yes, sir. Only Remi's going to be in a spot. He's going to have this castle—it wouldn't be nice to make his sons sleep out in a shed or something. So they'll have to grow up feeling rich. And the bigger you make the mine, the richer they'll feel. I reckon there's no help for it—he's going to have to lose 'em just like you did."

Misery got to his feet and began to pace up and down. "Now, skipper, you're gettin' things mixed up. We *got* to keep on expandin' the works—that's the natural—well, what in Sam Hill else do you do with a mine? And besides, money's a danged fine thing. Everybody could use more of it, unless you're a jackass-fool and—well, I sure enough ain't, but mebbe Remi is, and I better go up and have a talk with him."

Andy watched him go. He could see he'd got Misery upset and he hadn't meant to. Certainly hadn't meant to start another fuss between those two. It was just that he couldn't make some things balance in his own mind, and in talking it out loud he had somehow put his finger in the pot and stirred everybody up. Making things worse and worse. When he saw Josey coming in, he got up off the couch. At least he wasn't going to let her go upstairs and add to the fracas.

As she paused in the doorway he said grimly, "I was just coming outside—going to ask you if you'd care to take a little walk. Nice evening."

"Very nice." She considered him with her unfathomable dark eyes. "Yes, Andrew, I think I will go with you. There is a thing I need to know—you can explain." She tucked a hand through the crook of his arm and they strolled down the walk, turning along the road toward the mine by force of habit. "How does it happen you do not work?"

"Father allows me down the shaft only every other night."

"Ah, but you are learning about the dynamite."

"Some," he admitted cautiously.

"*Très bien.* Tell me!"

"What?"

"How it is to make the big explosion. I must know so that I, personally, can bring down that abominable old house."

"Gosh, Josey, I don't think they'll let you do it. Somebody might get hurt. Do people go around blowing up buildings in—well, in Paris?"

"Do not say anything against my France!" she warned him, with instant anger. "And do not think this —this village—is like Paris, *mon cher.*"

"Well, it pretty near will be when it gets a château of its own."

"Never, never!" She laughed scornfully, but suddenly there were tears in her eyes. "Paris is all green—

the beautiful boulevards, the parks. Everything is debonair—the lovely people move so slowly. . . ." She talked on, unfolding a picture of a city more handsome than any he had ever seen, of white marble buildings and a great cathedral that seemed to float in the midst of a sweeping river. As Andy listened he saw her face actually grow pretty with fondness and longing.

They had reached the mine now; the sun was half gone behind the hills to the west, sending long shadows aslant across the valley. The world seemed in a lull. Even Josey had lapsed into a wistful silence, and Andy was trying to screw up his determination to move closer to her, as they sat on the foot of the gallows frame. He had almost got his nerve up, when, underfoot, he sensed a dull thud, so faint that at first he couldn't figure what it was. A shot going off down in the depths of the mine? But it was too early in the evening. Hep never finished drilling at this hour. Josey hadn't even noticed. As she sat dreaming, Andy got up and roamed over to the main shaft, listening.

She glanced at him sadly. "Always with men, it is the work they love. Your heart is down in that ugly hole, is it not so?"

"Not quite," he said lightly, though he kept wondering about it. Something might have gone wrong down there. Not wanting to upset her, he went on carelessly, "Maybe I ought to stick around here a while and just watch out for high-graders. But it's getting chilly—I think you ought to be going along home. Remi might be worried."

"Yes," she said, "I will go. I can talk no more." She hardly seemed to care about gold now. He watched her walk off, head tilted forward mournfully, blond hair falling about her face. The sun had dipped from sight and dusk was settling fast.

When she was gone, Andy turned and went across the mine yard quickly. At the ventilator shaft he stopped and listened, but could hear no sound from below. More sure than ever that something must be haywire, he began to climb down the ladder.

At each hundred-foot level a crosscut had been made by the previous owner, each connected with the ventilator for air. So that when he stepped off the ladder at the second level, Andy was standing in a tunnel much like the one they were working down on fourth. He paused there, peering down the narrow hole. For now he could see that, far below on third, a candle was spiked into the wall. He could hear Hep moving around down there in the third-level tunnel, heard his dry cough—he was muttering to himself, so he was all right.

The smell of powder smoke reached Andy faintly. Evidently Hep had set off some small shot and was waiting for the fumes to clear before going back down to drill some more. Andy had never known his uncle to do it this way, but he certainly wasn't going to let him know that he'd been alarmed. He himself always hated to be fussed over. As quietly as possible he clambered back up the ladder to the surface.

Twilight had deepened in these last few minutes. He

paused in the gathering shadows, oddly uneasy. A stir of breeze rustled the dry grass—but there was no breeze! Flinging himself forward, he ducked instinctively, but a massive arm gripped him around the neck and another yanked his wrist behind his back, bending it upward sharply so that he had to bite down on a yelp. Struggling, he tried to twist loose, but couldn't break that grip. Couldn't yell, or even breathe. Steadily he was forced away from the airshaft.

"Now then"—a deep voice, he'd heard it before, twice in his life—"I'm going to let go. But keep still or I'll have to clout you." And abruptly he was released.

Choking with fury, Andy whirled to find that Duke had stepped back and was aiming a thin, pale shaft of light at him. It was coming from a metal cylinder— Andy had seen these flashlight things in the stores, but he'd never had one pointed at him before.

"So it's Billy's boy again," Duke was saying. "You must like the shades of night. Stay there!" He made a short gesture and Andy saw the gun in his other hand. The little black hole was pointed straight at him.

"What do you want?" he gasped hoarsely.

"Turn your pockets inside out. Quick now."

Half hypnotized by the spot of white light, Andy did as he was told. Dumped onto the ground his whole collection of odds and ends, knife, matches, and a few dollars. If Duke had turned holdup man, he thought bitterly, this was going to be lean pickings. But the sheriff left the money there. He seemed puzzled.

"Put your hands up." When Andy obeyed, Duke stepped forward and slapped lightly at his shirt and trousers as if seeking something hidden. "Nothing. But then what were you doing down that ladder?"

"It's my mine—partly. I can go down any time I want. Anyhow, what business is it of yours? Why do you keep hanging around? My father's not bothering you, why don't you leave him alone?" It came out in a random burst of pent-up resentment.

Duke almost laughed. There was cold ruthlessness in his voice as he said, "Why am I here? Pride and pocketbook, buck-o. It hurts both to buy a salted mine. Why, you could hardly imagine how irritated I was, a few years back, to find I'd bought five thousand dollars' worth of shotgun gold. I've been waiting a long time to square that."

"So you're—high-grading—from us!" It struck Andy like a thunderbolt.

Duke roared out loud that time. "Your father would enjoy this. No, laddy-buck, on the contrary—my star says I'm a deputy marshal of this county, authorized to seize and arrest such mischief-makers. Which I thought I was doing. But you can go. To accuse me—" He chuckled again. "Such innocence could hardly be counterfeit. Pick up that stuff and get yourself home."

By the baleful white light Andy collected his belongings.

"And when you get there, it will be as well—if you value that parent of yours, and you seem to—just as well to forget this little meeting tonight." Ungently he turned Andy around and started him on his way. "Don't come snooping up this hill again and don't send your father."

Twenty-one

Next night the depths of the mine seemed clammier and darker than ever. Andy thought that the shift would never end—possibly because it was his last time below ground with Hep. The two weeks were up and he was glad. As he served out those last hours, his eyes were burning with sleeplessness.

After the encounter with Duke last night he had gone home, ringing with the threat of those words. For hours he had lain awake, torn between wanting to tell his father and fear of getting him mixed up in a gun-fight with Duke. At last, some time in the early morning, he had decided it was too dangerous a secret to keep to himself and had tiptoed into the next bedroom, only to find it empty.

Nothing to do but go back to bed. For more hours he had held still, listening for every sound, imagining—

too many things. But a few thoughts had worked their way through the tangle of perplexity. As he relived the scene with Duke, one thing had come clear: The sheriff had grabbed him and searched him for just one reason —he must have thought Andy was the high-grader!

What else could he have been looking for? What else could he have meant by "innocence" when he let Andy go? He still couldn't imagine what interest Duke must have, to be trying so hard to catch a thief stealing somebody else's gold. Unless, of course, he was telling the truth—he wanted to settle an old personal wrong. But the people he thought had wronged him were the two Bretts, and yet Duke had seemed not to suspect Andy's father or even want him around the mine.

Which left only Hep. Could Duke be laying for *him?* He must have known Hep was below, if he'd kept watch all these nights. So if he had thought Andy was an accomplice, he must have suspected the two of them of plotting to smuggle ore out of the mine. It was ridiculous; Andy tried to laugh at the idea. But through the long hours of the night the joke had worn thin in spots. Questions of his own had kept rising. Now they were still all bottled up inside him. His head felt swollen; it throbbed every time Hep's sledge came down on the drill.

Wearily Andy hoped this would be the last hole— counted the ones already drilled; there were five. This would make the sixth, then, and he was almost through. When Hep stepped back at last, he, too, heaved a sigh.

"There it is, nephew. We'll pack our powder and then your days in this dungeon are over. Better hunt around for a scrap of picture-rock to prove to your grandchildren that you've dug gold."

"Except that I haven't really." Andy spoke absently. "Maybe tomorrow I'll ask Father to let me use the pick a little."

"Tomorrow?" Hep laughed oddly. "Tomorrow all this will be far behind you. You'll be speeding toward a new life. There, now, I've gone and given away my surprise. Your train ticket—I've bought it for you, my boy. The others are too busy to think of such details." He was tamping powder into the holes as he talked.

Andy was shocked. "But I didn't plan to go so soon! I mean—I've got more to learn."

"I can't imagine what. You've watched every step, seen every secret of the trade—"

"You never explained about setting off small shots," Andy remarked tentatively. "Didn't you do that last night—set off a little explosion about seven o'clock?"

For an instant Hep went stock-still. Then he glanced over his shoulder, smiling. Candlelight flashed off his glasses. Andy couldn't see the look of his eyes. "You're right, nephew! And very acute of you to catch it, though you shouldn't have been hanging around this dreary place on your evening off. Oh, the explanation is simple enough. I came to a hard area in the rock. Rather than exhaust myself by drilling deep, I made a few shallow holes and loosened the face of the drift a bit. Ah, it's a pity—to try to do expert work without power-driven tools."

It sounded logical enough. Andy felt a little embarrassed for having worked up a lot of foolish suspicions. Generously he said, "Father told me you know more about gold than anybody on earth. He said I'd learn a lot from you."

Hep looked flattered. "You're a good student, my boy, and if you ever come back to this country in later life, you'll not be a complete novice. Even years of schooling, such as Remi had, can't make a man an expert."

Andy was thinking that Duke Dade himself had once been so green he'd bought a worthless mine. Or *said* he had! It seemed hard to believe that a man like Duke could be that stupid. He was probably lying about the whole business—Andy would have felt relieved if that were true.

With rising hopes he said, "Father told me a mine could be sold to a tenderfoot just by sprinkling some false ore around the tunnel. But wouldn't a really smart man be able to tell the difference?"

Hep was moistening rock dust to close the holes. "Why, of course," he replied carelessly. "That would hardly fool an easterner fresh off the stage. The mine to watch out for is the one where no free gold at all is in sight. If a man invites you to break off a chunk from the face of the drift and have it assayed, be alert! Go at least a foot into the rock for your sample. Because a single load of gold chloride fired from a shotgun at short range will produce a rock face that assays like high-grade ore." He was going on about the chemistry of it. Andy lost track. For inside him his heart had fallen with a thud. Shotgun gold . . .

"And that'll—fool—anybody." He said it softly. All at once the drift seemed ominously still. Hep was bent over the fuses, tying them, fingers so adept . . . like the raccoon. The smartest little thief in the animal kingdom. The truth came over Andy almost gently. Instead of being aghast, he could only feel the same dismay and rueful affection he'd always felt when he caught his comical, furry little beast in some mischief. Hep! A salter of mines. Even, probably, a high-grader!

At that moment his uncle glanced up keenly. With an effort Andy tried to compose his face. He'd have to think what to do—talk this over with his father. They'd figure some way to put a stop to this without the others having to know.

"What is it, nephew? You look disturbed." Hep was still watching him.

"I was just thinking about—my father."

"You're a wise lad, to worry about Billy. He's an unhappy man. I'm sure you can understand how it is, to yearn for a beautiful, carefree existence with no responsibilities—every day a new adventure. Every night a new game. Gambling is the flavor of some men's lives—without it they lose their zest."

And for the first time Andy thought he did understand. What his uncle said about Will Brett was actually a picture of—Hep.

"Maybe Father never really liked to live that way. Adeline said he was lonesome—she said it would be hard on him if I left."

Hep sniffed. "Romantic imaginings! Women are weak creatures."

Andy would have put Adeline up against Uncle Hep, pound for pound. "Maybe he does need me though. At least I ought to stay around until I'm sure. I don't think I'd better leave yet."

Hep bent over his fuses again. "You may take those things out of the drift, lad. We're ready to shoot."

Lugging the drills and sledge around the corner into the main tunnel, Andy stacked them. After a slight delay Hep came along, unrolling the large fuse.

"There's only one drawback to lingering here," he was remarking, "and that's your school plans. Here it is, well into August—these things don't get arranged overnight, my boy. That's why I probably took too much upon myself and bought your ticket. First-class fare too." The fuse was lit and burning. Hep led Andy away from the drift, still going on about the train trip. "You've never eaten in a dining car, have you? Such luxury, to carve up a roast pheasant while the country-side glides past—"

The mighty blast shook the tunnel. As the reverberations died, Hep was still rattling on.

"—imagine reaching the East Coast, two thousand

miles away, in less than fifty hours! I wish I could see your face the first time you catch a glimpse of the ocean. Vaster than Kansas, my boy, and all water."

There was something wrong, something different tonight from their usual routine, but Andy couldn't think what it was, with Hep bubbling over this way. As they climbed the shaft he was still trying to place it. At the top of the first ladder he paused, holding the candle up to glance about him at the deserted third-level tunnel. Hep reached his side, huffing and coughing.

"What's the matter, nephew? Why stop?"

"I don't know—I was just wondering what this level was like." He walked a way along the crosscut, peering ahead. There in the shadows he caught sight of a comfortable little parlor set up—empty powder keg turned up for a table with a deck of cards on it, a candleholder, and some magazines. Gunny sacks full of something were placed to sit on. Hep must have waited for the smoke to clear from a small shot many a night, then gone down and picked through the rock fall for the bits of high grade before setting off his larger shot. It was all falling into place. But Andy didn't want to seem suspicious. Carelessly he said, "Why do you reckon there isn't any gold up on this level?"

"Still in the clutches of the fever, eh, lad?" Hep chuckled. "Haven't had your belly full of it yet? Well, perhaps it's this unfulfilled desire luring you on—the craving to strip aside the rock with a pick and lay bare the gleaming, virgin metal. I can understand your quest for such an experience. Who knows? You may even become a journalist someday and wish to set down these far-western experiences in a book. There's only one way to get the wish out of your system. Grab up a pick and try it. I'll wager a half-hour of it would satisfy you permanently."

"Maybe so," Andy agreed. He was trying to figure what he would do when they reached the surface if Duke were there. He hadn't bothered them on other nights when they came off-shift together. If he'd just hold off this once more, Andy could see his father alone and they would deal with Uncle Hep quietly. Make him pay back the money from the stolen ore and—

"Nephew?"

With a start, Andy roused. He realized Hep had asked him some question he had missed. As they emerged into the cool night air up top, he fumbled apologetically. "I'm sorry. I was—I was—"

"Thinking again? Never mind—I understand. All I suggested was that I'd try to help you with your experiment." Suddenly Hep's voice was nervous, as if he were upset, or even frightened. "I doubt that your father would tolerate any practicing by a mere boy, when profits are at stake. But if you'd care to meet me here tomorrow morning early, before the others come to work, I'll be glad to show you the knack. It should be somewhat of a thrill for you, personally, to hack off a piece of the choicest picture-rock, to keep as a souvenir of this summer's adventure. Is it a bargain?"

It occurred to Andy that this was a useful idea. Hep always went into town after work these nights, usually didn't get home until morning. That would give Andy time to speak to his father alone. They could come back together and meet Hep at the mine early, settle the business in privacy. It would mean that Hep would have to go away somewhere and promise to lead an honest life.

Sadly he said, "All right, sir. Tomorrow morning. I'll be here."

Twenty-two

It was still dark when the alarm went off. Andy fought his way up out of a restless sleep. But with consciousness came the memory of the task ahead, jolting him wide awake. Flipping back the bedclothes, he padded across noiselessly in his bare feet to the door of his father's room. He'd been out when Andy got home. Listening now, he still heard no sound of breathing. Striking a match, he saw at a glance that his bed was unoccupied. It was the one thing he hadn't figured out, in his weary state last night—what he would do if his father never did come home.

Of course there was a chance he'd find him over on Squaw Mountain somewhere—maybe stalking Duke. Andy dressed quickly. Birds were beginning to twitter as he went downstairs quietly and out into the fresh cold mountain morning air. There was just enough light coming in the eastern sky for him to make his way along the road at a good clip. Turning off up the side of the hill, he made a swift circuit of the route that he and his father had taken home that night, coming out at Josey's rock. No one in sight.

He went on to the mine. The shack was locked, nobody hiding around the pile of timbers. It seemed unnaturally quiet on every side. Over east, a strip of lemon-yellow light rimmed the mountains. Against it, the shaft house of the old abandoned mine rose stark and black.

In the stillness the sound of a short, hacking cough startled him. Andy whirled to find that Hep had just stepped up out of the ventilator. It seemed strange—that he had come back and gone down there again. He was waving.

"Good morning, nephew."

And now a momentary indecision seized Andy. To leave—make some excuse and put this off until later? But that might set Hep to wondering. Better to go through the motions and just hope that his father would be the first one down the shaft when they all came to work. He went over reluctantly to join his uncle. At the back of his mind something still hovered—an uneasiness about the routine last night. He hadn't placed it yet.

"You're early, my boy. Excellent." But Hep's voice was hoarse and strained; his cough much worse than usual. "After a night's sleep I trust you've got some clearer thoughts on the subject of your future. I've always felt you had a good head—"

"I haven't changed my mind," Andy told him with a touch of irritation. "Thank you, anyhow, but there are still things to be settled here."

Hep looked at him oddly. "Settled? Few things ever are really settled, lad. But perhaps we can put an end to one, at least, eh? Let's go below."

As they climbed down the ladder Andy's apprehension grew stronger. Hard to say why—you certainly couldn't be afraid of a jolly little man like Hep. Trying so hard to sell the Atlantic Ocean last night—

Abruptly it struck Andy, the thing that had escaped him. Hep had talked right through the explosion of shot. He hadn't listened to it at all. But Andy had—with some inner part of his mind. It came to him now what was wrong. Only five of the charges had gone off. He was almost certain of it, now that he thought back. And all the while his uncle had been gabbing as if it didn't matter.

He was breezing along now, so volubly it made it hard to think. Talking about schools, studies, culture—everything under the sun. Something kept telling Andy that it had a meaning, all this conversation. As they reached the third level he glanced around. Nothing to see, except a small metal box with wires attached to it and a handle on top. It glinted dully in the light—a small box—must have missed it last night. And then as they went down the last ladder Hep grew suddenly silent, and the mine seemed to close in around them, tightening like a living presence.

At the bottom fumes still hung faintly in the air. They seemed to aggravate Hep's cough. Choking and gasping, he went forward to the tool room near the main shaft and brought back a pick; the two of them walked into the drift. Jamming his candlestick into a crack, Andy surveyed the wreckage left by last night's shot. Loose rock hung in ragged chunks along the walls, and the floor was a shambles of rubble.

"You could pick up a piece of good ore in that," Hep said, glancing down at it, "but the idea is to learn to use this tool. Don't drive too hard at first, get the feel of the rhythm. Like this." He took a swing and brought down some loose rock. "Aim for the cracks, try to break off chunks. Start over there and you'll lay bare some of our wealth—" A spasm of coughing shook him. He handed over the pick. "Go ahead—try it. I must get a breath of clearer air."

Andy hefted the tool. The spot that Hep had indicated was a jutting edge—part of the face of the drift that the blast hadn't knocked down. Cracked and crumbling, it stood there inviting him to smash it. But surely Hep should have known that was dangerous? Or had he really forgot to count the shot last night? It was such a terrible thought—to suppose that he might be doing this on purpose! Andy turned to see his uncle going down the drift quickly, almost running. His father's warning flashed across his mind. *Don't leave Hep's side when you're below!*

"Uncle," he called, "will you be back right away? I'd like to ask you something."

Reluctantly the little man stopped and returned a few steps. "What is it, nephew?"

"About these shots you set last night—are you sure they all went off?"

"Yes, yes, of course." Hep turned away again.

"Could you—would you mind coming back here a minute?" As Hep returned slowly, frowning, Andy began to examine the cracked face of rock more closely, almost certain now what he was looking for. "Here it is!" An end of fuse clipped short, only a little of it showing. "Do you reckon there could be a live shot under there? I thought I only heard five go off last night."

"Nonsense, lad. You know that I count shot very carefully. Your ears just aren't used to it yet, that's all." Hep had halted ten feet away.

Quickly Andy drew back the pick as if to swing. "All right, then, I'll—"

"*Stop!*" The word broke from Hep like a scream. Hastily he backed off. "I've—I've just noticed—your pick has a crack in it—head might come loose and fly off—I'll go—go—" The words died. Because Hep was caught in his own trap and he knew it. He knew that Andy knew it too. His whole starchy manner collapsed, the stoutness draining out of him, leaving him sagging like a soft balloon.

"You're a clever boy, nephew"—his voice came thin and sickly—"you're like your father, quick to observe. What was it tipped you? The small explosion? Or my careless instructions on how to salt a mine? No matter —you've driven me into this. I've got no choice—no choice—" Step by step he was moving back toward the main tunnel, Andy following cautiously. By the time they'd reached the end of the drift they were circling each other, wary as two animals.

"Then you did leave a shot there, to go off when I hit it," Andy muttered numbly, still finding it hard to believe.

Hep's eyes were shining wildly behind his glasses—a look that Andy had seen more than once in a cornered thing. "I told Billy in the beginning it was bad luck to bring a kid into the game. Bad for him and me and bad for you. I don't see why he had to do it—everything was good before. Why didn't you go? I did all I could—" He half stumbled over the equipment which Andy had left just at the mouth of the drift, and snatched up a sledge. Almost hysterically he yelled, "Stay where you are! I foresaw this might happen—the way you stared at me last night, your lying little excuses. 'My father needs me.'" He tittered terribly. "Your father will be well off without you, you little idiot, meddling—" And then his look stretched past Andy, his jaw went slack and the hand with the hammer fell to his side.

It was Will Brett himself moving out of the shadows near the main shaft. At he walked forward, the light of the candles showed his high-boned face, stern as a judge's.

"Billy . . . *Billy!*" Hep's voice rose to a wail of anguish. "Oh, no! I thought he might tip one of the others, but not *you!* Why did you—? Oh, no! No!"

"Nobody tipped me, Hep. I've been watching you every night since we struck pay-rock."

"Why? *Why did you have to mix into this?*" the little man screeched.

"Did you think I'd cover up for you on such a thing? Stealing from our own partners? No, Hep. I've had enough. I should have put a stop to your pranks way back in the beginning. All these years I've protected you, supported you, made an honest living for us both so that you wouldn't be tempted to cheat. I've pretended your petty theft was harmless—I thought maybe you'd get over it and grow into a man. I wouldn't even believe you had really salted a mine—not until I talked to Duke a while back. He told me some things that set me thinking."

"You believe him—against me?"

"You made a mistake when you used his name to call the Mine Owners' Association and spoil my chances for work. Some of them know him and word got back—that's what brought him down here, to find out who it was."

"Not me—!"

"Yes, you. It had to be. Though where you got the money for a long-distance call—? It was from Andy's knapsack, wasn't it? Did you really steal from a kid, Hep?"

"It was a good life before he came—" Hep was almost crying.

"It was a rotten, shiftless life with no point to it. We were lucky to get the chance to make a good honest haul in this mine. We could have made enough stake to go our separate ways—"

"I've got some! Billy, I've got quite a bit set aside, up on the third level. Billy, we can get out of here—"

"On stolen goods? After you tried to get my son to blow himself to bits? Great guns, Hep! That's murder!"

The reality of it hit Andy all at once and he sank onto one of the powder kegs dizzily. Everything had happened so fast, only now did the truth get home to him.

"What are you—?" Hep was whining. "You wouldn't let 'em send me away—"

"I've been intent on catching you for weeks; I was going to turn you over to the law. Now I feel like settling things with my own hands." For all his coldness Brett was more furious than Andy had ever seen a man.

"Keep back, Billy!" Hep had a gun in his hand. "I'll do it! You won't turn me over to a sheriff—never!"

"You're making matters worse, Hep. Put that away."

"I'm going out of here! Don't try to follow or I'll shoot." Wildly he dashed to the ladder and scrambled up into the air vent.

Brett slumped a little. His hands unclenched and he

came back to Andy's side. "Are you all right?" He put a hand on Andy's shoulder gently as a man might touch a valuable possession. "When I heard what you and Hep were saying just now, I got weak inside."

"Where were you?" Andy asked shakily.

"I've been waiting for weeks to discover what he's been doing with the ore—never thought of the third level as a possibility. Anyhow after he stayed down here all night, I decided to climb down the shaft on a rope. I must have started down just before you got here—"

"All night?" Andy shook his head to clear it. Some hunch was trying to get through. "I think we'd better get out of here."

"He won't get very far. No use in our running such a risk. In that airshaft a gun would be deadly."

"I think we'd better try it." Andy stood up, and as he did, the powder keg tipped over. He knew what was the matter. He had sensed as he sat on it that it was empty. "These"—he tried another one, and it was empty, too—"these are supposed to be full."

Quick to seize the idea, Brett yanked the candle from the wall and held it down lower. On both sides of the tunnel, wires lay along the floor. Andy let out a short breath of relief.

"Those aren't fuses."

"They could be. Electric fuses. If he's got a dry-cell battery somewhere—"

"There was a little metal box up on third level," Andy began.

His father seized his arm. "Quick, head for the shaft!" As they ran forward they could see the fuses snaking everywhere. "He's got the whole tunnel wired!" Brett was hauling Andy back the other way. "We'll have to chance the ventilator—" But the fuses were there, too, coming out of the walls.

"Couldn't we cut 'em?"

"No time. Into the drift!" As they ran, headlong, suddenly the whole earth seemed to heave around them. Andy was flung down, swallowed by a sea of terrible, earsplitting noise, falling rock, and then, darkness.

Twenty-three

For a few seconds Andy couldn't get his lungs to work. Painfully he struggled in the dark, got a gulp of air, and choked on acrid smoke. As he lay there, choking, ears still roaring, he could feel the fine grit settling on his face. Burying his head in the crook of his arm, he managed to breathe in short, shallow gasps. As his senses cleared he could hear his father moving, somewhere nearby, strangling on powder fumes. Struggling up onto hands and knees, he crawled toward the sound.

"Son . . . ?" A groping hand found his arm. "Are you hurt?"

"I'm all right." Andy choked again.

"Get back—to the far end." The hand urged him away from the mouth of the drift. Groggily Andy got to his feet and fumbled along a few steps in the pitch black. Then a match flared and he saw his father, a ghostly figure in the haze of smoke. He was searching for the candle—found it and got it lit. The yellow flame was veiled in curling fumes, but enough light cut through to show that the main tunnel was a tight pack of fallen rock. The mouth of the drift was blocked solidly.

Getting slowly to his feet, Brett stared at it, then followed Andy along the drift. When they reached the ore face they found the air a little clearer. All around them it was quiet—the blunted stillness of a sealed tomb. For a minute neither said anything. Andy thought sickly that, for once, it was just as well he couldn't tell what his father was thinking. A fine sweat stood out on Brett's lean, hard face. But when he spoke his voice was almost even.

"I'm sorry. This is my fault."

"No! It was me he wanted to get rid of."

"My fault—from years back. But especially I should never have put you down here. I knew what he was up to, I planted you with him to make sure. It went as I thought—since you've been coming to work every other night, there's been a difference in the yield from day to day. It told me all I needed to know. But this—I didn't expect." He broke off, swallowing hard.

Andy tightened against his own inner trembling. "How long you figure it'll take 'em to dig us out?"

"Too long. We're not going to sit here and wait." He was eying the pick that lay where Andy had dropped it. But to hack at that wall of broken granite by hand seemed so futile it only made Andy sweat harder. His father walked over and plucked the candle out of the wall. "With mine that gives us about ten hours of light."

"I've got a little piece in my pocket."

"Ten and a half, then. Maybe more if we catch the wax." Stooping, he found a fragment of rock that had a natural hollow in it and stuck his candle to it with some hot drippings. Then, collecting the pick, he started forward again into the thick of the fumes. "You stay here."

Andy bit back a protest. Tensely he waited while the flicker of light receded, was almost lost in the haze. He could just make out that his father had reached the rock fall and was passing the candle across the face of the debris slowly, up and down, back and forth. . . .

At last Brett called hoarsely, "Andy, I need you."

With a deep breath he plunged forward into the fumes. Coming to his father's side, he said, "Yes, sir?" But the words sounded like a rasp of fear.

"See if you notice anything—or am I imagining it? Damnable smoke's blurred my eyesight." Brett held the candle out, moving it painfully slow. At one point he stopped—the flame seemed to waver as if the least little draft had stirred it.

"It's fluttering," Andy agreed.

"Good. Means that air is coming in. The pack must be looser right there." He took the pick. "This will go faster if you hold the light. Can you stand it?"

Andy nodded. He was afraid his voice would give him away. His throat was raw, eyes beginning to water and burn. As he stood with the candle clamped hard in both hands, trying not to gag on the bitter fumes, he was thinking that Hep had gone through this every night, just to get more than his fair share of gold. He wondered if he would ever understand that. Not that he was going to be around long enough to understand much more of anything.

"I'll bet they think we're dead," he muttered. "Maybe they won't even try to get us out."

His father squinted at him through the smoke. "They'll try. But don't dwell on that. See if you can figure . . . where this air may be . . . coming from." He spoke in spurts between blows of the pick. "I'm striking wood . . . timbers . . . that east wall was right across from here. Must have caved in toward us. Always was weak . . . only bad spot in the tunnel. Suggest anything to you?"

"No, sir."

"You sound shaky, son. If the fumes start to get you, put the candle on the floor and go back. I can manage."

But Andy could see that it took all the light they had for the skillful job his father was doing. Deftly widening the little cracks, driving hard into the bigger ones, he loosened whole cascades of stone.

With strained humor Andy said, "I reckon I'll stay here. I always did want a lesson in how to use a pick."

Brett paused to shake the damp hair back out of his eyes. A smile broke across his face for an instant—a small gesture of reassurance. "Remember the night we walked away from Duke's shotgun?"

"I was scared then too." Andy grinned back feebly.

"You didn't falter once. That's when I started being proud that you were my son." Abruptly he turned and swung the pick again as if embarrassed by the confession.

"Proud—of me?" Andy repeated awkwardly.

"I know—I didn't show it. Couldn't. All those years" —rock crashed down—"waiting and wishing I could see you. Then to have it happen that way. No use to swear I was innocent; a man who'll cheat will lie about it. But I vowed I wouldn't let you down. And I won't —not if I can help it."

Wordlessly Andy watched his father throw his strength at the granite barricade. And as he stood there, while time burned lower and lower, he felt a deep, wondering, helpless pain. To know—too late probably—that here was all he had ever wanted. That he had come home.

After hours of the ring of pick against stone, the sudden silence was full of echoes.

"Candle." Brett held out his hand for it. Andy stood back, blinking. He had been staring at the flame for so long it left spots in front of his eyes. But it was easier than looking at the walls of their cell. Even the cavity his father had made in the rubble was so small—only a couple of feet deep.

He was bending down, exploring it with the light.

The flame shivered noticeably now. "Air—come through here." He pointed to a loose jumble of rock and splintered timbering. Glancing over his shoulder he added, "It's driving the fumes back too."

Which was true. They could see each other better. Even though his head throbbed like a pump, Andy realized he wasn't coughing so much. "Which way is it coming from?"

Brett shook his head. "I can't figure it. It's too steady to be seeping through much rock." He gave the candle back and went to work again. Andy sensed more purpose in it now. The work was going faster—every time Brett pried loose a timber, the rock around it came down in a small avalanche. The niche was deepening. And then the pick struck hard against something solid and he swore.

Andy held the light higher while his father scraped away some debris. What they saw brought them both to a dead standstill. When the east wall had crashed, three huge boulders had wedged. On either side other massive chunks blocked the way. It would take a man days to hack through a heavy spot like that by hand. Brett hunkered down to study the problem, his face troubled. He was holding a hand in front of a small hole formed where the three largest rocks came together.

"Here's the source of our air. Not a trace of smoke in it, either." Taking the light, he tried to peer into the opening. "Deep. I can't make out the far side. Either a cave or it could be a drift from the old mine. These hills

214

are honeycombed with tunnels. That must have been what weakened the east wall. If we could get through to it—" The candle guttered and went out.

In the darkness, panic rose inside Andy. He had to force himself to stand quiet while his father was busy with something—he heard cloth tear. And then Brett struck a match; they had light again. He had taken a scrap from his shirttail and twisted it into a wick. Stuck in the pool of candle wax, it made a flame that was fitful, but enough to see by. Andy took it with trembling hands while his father still stood and pondered their problem.

He himself couldn't think about it. He kept trying to imagine what he would do when the last candle was used up and they were left in that final darkness. How long would it take to get it over with—no food or water —how was he going to act? Keep thinking about being rescued—that was all you could do. He tried to picture Misery, probably over there right now on the other side of the rock fall, working to get them out. Adeline would be bringing lunch soon—she'd be pretty upset. And Remi would be beside himself. He might even have hired a man or two to help. He'd want to get to the drift and the gold as quickly as possible. . . .

"There's one thing we've got to do," he said distantly, just an extension of his thoughts.

Brett didn't look up. "What's that?"

"I was just thinking, when we find—I mean if the time comes that we know we—I mean, before the last

215

candle goes out, we ought to leave them a note. About that live shot back there. You wouldn't want Misery or somebody to drive a pick into it."

"The shot?" His father swung around, staring. With sudden fierceness he seized Andy by the shoulders. "I forgot the shot! That's what we need—powder! Sitting snug in its hole, waiting to be pulled out and used! Great guns, that's it, son!"

And now they worked feverishly. To bite into that granite would take tempered steel—they dug for Hep's tools. Only a foot or two inside the tunnel, but it meant hours of wracking effort. Andy took a turn with the pick while his father went back to scoop the powder out of the death trap. It was hard work, but he was bringing down rubble at a pretty good clip. In the uneven light of the burning wax he got a glimpse of something shiny. Pulled it out—a star drill.

Before the hole for the powder was finished, the second candle had burned down half its length. Andy didn't mention it though. His father's complete thought was focused on the mechanics of setting the blast. They were going to try to break up the bottom rock, hoping the other two would continue to brace each other and hold back the rest of the pack. As they finally lay flat at the far end of the drift, waiting for the fuse to burn its course, the seconds pounded past a heartbeat at a time.

When it came, the booming explosion seemed muted and lonely, far short of the huge, splintering impact of a big multiple blast. But the bottom rock was broken. Split in a dozen pieces of a size to handle. Watching the upper structure, Brett began delicately to pry the fragments loose with one of Hep's tools. Little by little he enlarged the small opening to the size of a fist, then to the size of a man's head. By the end of another hour it was almost twice as big, with a yawning darkness beyond that they still couldn't probe with the light.

Pausing to wipe the sweat out of his eyes, Brett glanced at Andy. "Think you could get through there?"

"I might. But you couldn't."

"Take a look."

Sensing a new tautness in his father, he put his head into the opening and saw what the trouble was. Beyond the rock that the powder had splintered was another—too big to move and too far in to go to work on.

"I can chip at it," Brett went on, "but the going will be slow and we've got less than half an hour of light left. If that's the old mine, over there, it may take every scrap of candle we've got for you to search a way out."

Andy pulled back out of the hole fast and straightened up to stare at his father aghast.

"It can't be helped," Brett said quietly. "It's not an inviting task, but you'll have to try it. When you lead the rescue party in, don't forget to bring along more powder."

Put up to him that way Andy could only nod. But his heart was racing as he began to worm his way into the hole, holding his breath, wriggling to get his shoulders through the ragged opening. He felt his father grab his belt and shove. Shirt tore and skin scraped, but his shoulders were through. Feeling his way, he dragged himself over the big rock, his hips broke loose, and he tumbled onto a rocky floor.

Brett handed the candle through the hole. "What have we got into?"

"It's an old drift all right." Andy looked around. "They must have dug right up to here and stopped."

"They were probably following the same rock structure that we've been working on. Follow it back—it will lead you to a crosscut. When you get there, follow an air current, try to find a ventilator with a ladder up it. Remember the wood will be old. Test every rung before you put your weight on it."

As his father talked Andy looked off into that blackness ahead, trying to listen, trying to brace up and answer steadily. "Yes, sir."

"Watch your candle—let it guide you. The more air, the faster it will burn so you'd better get started. Don't worry about me. And don't lose your head—thank the Lord you've got a good, steady one."

The words haunted Andy as he started off down the drift. Almost at once black shadows closed in around him, ahead and behind the small circle of light. His steps echoed in the empty silence of a lifeless place. When he reached the crosscut, it seemed to stretch off to eternity in both directions. He thought he'd better mark the spot and left his knife stuck upright in one of the ties of the old track that lay along the floor of the tunnel. Then, holding his candle up, he watched the thread of smoke critically.

It eddied toward the right. He followed it, past other drifts—some short, some reaching away out of sight. One had track laid along it, but he passed that up and followed the candle flame. Far along he felt the circulation grow stronger and, looking up, found the ventilator—without a sign of ladder. Trying not to falter under the defeat, he turned back the way he had come. The next best chance was probably the drift where the track was laid.

By now his candle was at its last flicker. He felt in his pocket and found the remaining short stub. Less than an inch. All that stood between him and final, unbroken darkness. Hurrying, he searched for the drift and turned along it. It seemed to lead on forever, but he began to feel a flow of air, though now he was moving against it instead of with it. No matter, if it led him to a way up. Ahead he saw that the track ended. Just as well that he slowed down, for abruptly the tunnel ended, too, in a vast gaping void. He stood on the verge of a huge vault, thirty feet across, falling away below, yawning above him higher than the candlelight could reach.

He had heard enough mine talk to guess what it was: a stope. A monster of a stope, the pocket left when a vein is mined out. Cautiously he tossed a rock into the black depths and listened . . . listened. . . . Nothing. A bottomless pit once filled with rich ore, now just a place for the wind to whisper. Air was coming into this vast man-made cavern from somewhere above. Since miners had once crawled the walls to knock down the ore, there should be ladders. None close by, but he did find a ledge hewn in the rock that led off around the face of the stope. Holding his breath, Andy ventured along it, pressed close against the damp rock.

The narrow catwalk ended halfway around, and there he found what he was looking for. Half rotten, missing some of its rungs, it was a ladder, and it led upward into the dark reaches above. With his heart in his throat, Andy started to climb.

Didn't dare look back, or even think about "down." Think upward . . . about air . . . think about a man sitting in darkness, relying on you. "Proud that you were my son." All along, close enough to touch each other. Andy hadn't cried since he was a baby, but right now he felt like it. Clinging to the clammy ladder, gripping his candle, needing all his wits, he scorned himself harshly and the lump in his throat went away. Slowly he reached for the next rung; his hand met empty space. Felt higher—nothing. Raising his candle, he looked up, fearfully, then groaned aloud in relief. He had climbed a hundred feet, reached another level—he was on the lip of another tunnel. Hauling himself over the edge, he sat shivering a minute.

The air was much fresher here—no doubt of it any more. Losing no more time, he followed it. Another air vent—and this time a ladder. Climbing rapidly, he passed another level and then there it was—daylight. Right over his head. Andy crawled out into the clean air, slumped down on the ground with his face on his arms—the grass smelled so good he could have eaten some of it.

Sitting up at last, he looked around to get his bearings. He was near the old mine shaft. Just over the curve of the hill he could see the gallows frame of the *Sidewinder*. Getting to his feet, he picked up the last bit of his candle affectionately—thought he'd just save that—and started over the hill.

When he reached the crest a strange scene met his eyes. Down there by the shed a hundred people or more were gathered in the long shadows of the afternoon. Overhead the wheel was racing—he saw the skip come bursting up from below—a half-dozen men stepped off wearily. Adeline hurried over carrying a coffeepot while other men crowded onto the skip and down it plunged. Misery seemed to be running things. And there was Remi—at least it looked like Remi, under the rock dust. He must have actually been down there with them, digging!

As it came home to Andy that all this was for their rescue, he began to run down the slope. He could hardly wait to see Josey's face.

Twenty-four

"Such a beautiful funeral it would have been!" Josey lamented. "All white—six white horses pulling a snow-white hearse. I had it planned to the last little rosebud. Ah, it was going to be *magnifique!* You will never again have such a chance, *mon cher* Andrew."

"I hope not. At least not for a long time." He passed his plate to her. "I'd like some more eggs, please."

In spite of some lingering headache from the powder smoke and a few patches of scraped skin he felt good. Better than ever in his life, he thought. As the whole family sat around the breakfast table that next morning, he kept glancing across at his father. Almost always he met a look coming back. Late last night, when they had finally got Will Brett out, and he had stared up at the giant stope that Andy had scaled, his arm had come across his son's shoulders in a wordless fellowship that grew stronger now each time their eyes met.

After a night's sleep some of the haggard look had eased in Brett's face, though he was still grave as he talked about Hep.

"His worst trouble has always been an aversion to work. He would labor twice as hard as the next man to get out of having to take an ordinary honest job. With his schooling he could have done many things. When we first came here I tried to get him to apply for a job in a bank—"

Andy choked on a piece of bacon.

"—he's quick with figures, and good with a pen. But he'd have none of it. All he could think of was the day when we would both go back to 'playing the game,' as he called it."

"The way he played it, he'd have got you lynched too," observed Duke. With his big hat off he looked more human. His handsome face was tinged with good humor as if he were pleased with himself. The others treated him with respect; Andy was still leery. And yet they said Duke had worked as hard as any man to dig them out yesterday.

"They'd have strung you up in Black Hawk that night, Billy," he went on, "if I hadn't kept law and order. I still can't see why he would rig a game so that the blame would fall on you—even tip me off so I'd be on hand. Of course, I didn't know who passed the word."

"He wanted me to be run out of town," Brett said. And again he glanced at Andy. "He wanted to keep me from meeting a certain stagecoach. But it's the first time he ever tried any of his tricks in any game I was dealing, so I didn't suspect him myself. I knew somebody was switching decks on me but never had time to discover who it was."

Misery snorted in disgust. "Trustin' your family, just because they're your blood kin, can sure git ye into trouble."

Remi seemed mystified. "I still do not comprehend—this unfortunate man even tried to blame you for the destruction of our mine, Billee."

"Yes-sir-ree," Misery marveled. "He tried to tell us he caught you high-gradin' and you pulled a gun and he had to shoot at you and hit a powder keg and that's what brung the whole works down. Lordy, what a liar!"

Brett rubbed his brow as if his head still ached.

"What he didn't know," Duke said with satisfaction, "was that the local sheriff and me was onto him all along. Seen him slipping into the offices of a fence in town—an assayer who's been under suspicion. We were just waiting for him to go there again so's we could pick 'em both up. So the minute I felt the earth heave down below, I knew some mischief was afoot. And when Hep climbed up that ladder alone I had a hunch what he'd done. I didn't let him fast-talk me out of clapping the cuffs on him. Y'know, Billy, you could press a charge of attempted murder."

Brett's poker face was steady, but Andy saw the twinge of hurt in his eyes. "Has he—hasn't he said anything about our coming out of it alive?"

"Well, yes . . ." Duke seemed puzzled. "Matter of fact, when I dropped by the jail last night to tell him, instead of getting sicker at the news, which I'd expected, he seemed kind of relieved. You reckon he's some sorry he went that far?"

Will nodded. "Let's hope so. I'd have no heart to make things worse for him than they already are. As it is, he'll probably be sentenced to a number of years—?"

"Ten, at least. Ten long years at the state pen bustin' rock. Thieving and dynamiting private property are two things the judges lean hard on around here. May I have some more flapjacks, Miss Adeline, ma'am? I swear they're the best I've eaten since I left home in Iowa."

She smiled and blushed, pretty as a farm girl. Andy still couldn't get over her. All the red curls were gone, though she'd had to cut her hair mighty short to get rid of the dye. All this while it must have been growing out under the dust cap. Now, soft and brown and real, it looked fine tied up with that blue ribbon. Andy noticed that Duke kept staring at her, too.

"You'll be welcome to some more any time, Sheriff," she said warmly. "When Misery and me open our boardinghouse maybe you'll stay here when you come to town."

"I've been thinking I ought to move down here bag and baggage," Duke said genially. "This district is the biggest mess of grifters I ever saw. Makes me itch to get at 'em."

"What's this about a boardinghouse?" Brett asked.

Misery reached for the syrup. "Just decided it yesterday, Bill. The dang mine's been bringin' on my catarrh again. I had enough. And Addie here says she don't care if she never hears of a gold mine again."

"That's when I thought you boys were goners." She looked fondly at Andy. "With the whole bottom of the shaft caved in, I thought we'd never make it to you in time, even if you were alive. I turned sick of the whole business."

"I confess," Remi put in slowly, "that I, too, felt as if this *Sidewinder* had a poisoned fang. It gave me great grimness to work in this hole in the ground, to think of two men buried alive. And as I work I think: I will sell this mine. With your permission, of course—you are all partners."

Brett looked up. "Count me out of the partnership. My share in this was canceled out by what Hep's done. I wish I could pay you all back for the ore he stole."

"No, no, we have recovered a great deal of it—" Remi began.

"Not only that, but if I'd not delayed, in order to be certain, if I'd worked with Duke, we might have brought him to book before he wrecked the mine. I feel that's my fault." As they started to protest he smiled, a short, grateful smile that transformed his brooding face. "Thanks for your generosity, but I'm through with the business. Andy and I are moving on. Today."

"And we"—Josey's eyes were bright with excitement—"we will do this 'moving on' also, Remi? Back to France, perhaps?"

He nodded. "There were several offers made yesterday. If you agree, I will sell and divide the profits. Let someone else reopen the shaft. For me it is—what is the word?—a caved-in dream."

Josey leaned over to whisper ecstatically to Andy. "Ah, but he does not tell all. After the old papa talked and talked, that night when I came back from walking with you, my brother slipped away up to the attic. He found the music box—I do not know how—and for a long time he listened. I think then he knew we must go back to France!"

And with the mine settled, a relief seemed to come over them all. Andy glanced around at them—gay as kids at a picnic. It was a weight off his mind that no real harm had come from all his fumbling. He felt glad for them. But it was a distant thing, as if he were a long way off, looking back at the scene. He glanced at his father; Brett was staring into his coffee cup. And whether the others could have guessed, at least Andy knew what was going on in his mind. A certain sadness that one person was missing. The crusher had claimed one victim. And he, too, felt a pang of grief for Uncle Hep.

As they walked toward town an hour later Andy felt as if the past two months were slipping away behind them like a dream. Glancing over, as one partner to another, he said to his father, "Where's the next stop?"

Brett's face was blank as the sky. "Who knows?"

Andy felt a little disappointed. He had hoped the mystery would be over between them. And now his father was pretending they didn't have any plans, and yet Andy knew he had gone downtown early this morning. Must have been to buy them tickets to somewhere.

"We could try the West Coast," Brett went on. "Texas, maybe. Alaska. Or maybe you want to go to Virginia and be a gentleman."

And then Andy knew it was his father's way of teasing. "They might turn me into a lawyer. I reckon I'm not cut out for that."

"Well, it's certain they wouldn't let you be a horse doctor."

Andy gaped in sheer astonishment. "That's what you wanted to be!"

"I scandalized them. Instead of riding out to hunt foxes, I spent my time in the stables. Just wasn't done around those parts. You never were supposed to get your hands very dirty."

Fervently Andy said, "I like to fool with animals too."

"Ever do much with horses?" They happened to be going down the street where the livery stable was. A couple of saddled horses were standing tied out in front. Brett jerked a thumb toward them. "I'd say those would

228

carry a man farther for the price than he could afford to go by train."

"Maybe we ought to ask about it!"

Brett walked over critically, passed the handsome sorrel, and ran a hand down the neck of the sleek black mare. Suddenly untying the reins, he handed them to Andy. "Her name is Cricket."

With his surprise a success, the mysterious manner left Will Brett and his face relaxed. For the first time in months some of the fine lines eased. As they rode east from Victor he shoved the hat back on his head, so that the noon sun fell on his face.

"You know," he remarked, "we're not exactly rich."

Andy wasn't worried—not with this horse under him. He could hardly take his eyes off the beautiful curve of her shoulder, the sturdy way she dug in as they climbed the crest of the mountain. Dropping away behind were the gallows frames and smokestacks of Cripple Creek. The grinding of the crushers was lost now; here was only the clean sound of the wind sifting through the foxtail pine.

"At the last minute," his father went on, "Remi insisted I take my share for the last two weeks' work— brings our total worth to a couple of thousand dollars. When that's gone, I think I can make us a living. Feel like working out under the sun for a while—maybe we can find a farmer who needs help with his harvest. The one thing I won't do, though, is to gamble again—that's a sworn promise. You'll never have reason to call my money 'dirty.' That day I pawned my gun, I was desperate—it only brought ten dollars. So I did go to the poker house—I guess you must have seen me there. Won a few hundred and almost lost my son."

Andy kept still. He just hoped his father would never know what he really had thought for a while.

"Now," Brett was going on, "I can go and see your grandfather with a clear conscience. I think we ought to stop by and see him—he must be worried about you. I'd like him to know that you're well and safe. How would that suit you?"

If anything could have made Andy feel better, that idea did. Wordlessly he nodded.

"Good. I don't think we'll disagree on many things. I've an idea we're two of a kind; even though we may be a fairly small pair right now, there's time ahead of us." Brett leaned back in the saddle comfortably. "Whatever schooling you decide you want, we'll manage it. In fact no matter what trade or profession you choose, you can be certain I'll never stand against it."

"Even horse doctoring?" Andy grinned across at him. For he had been thinking of the million little creatures that needed help. In fact, beyond that, if you could ever figure them out, there were—people.

The trees were thinning now; they had come through to the eastern face of the mountains. Ahead, the plains stretched off as far as Andy could see. The whole world spreading out around them and there weren't any s to it—none at all.

Format by Robin Ward
Set in linotype Janson
Composed, printed and bound by American Book-Stratford Press
HARPER & ROW, PUBLISHERS, INCORPORATED